KT-232-536

THE ADVENTURES OF MR. VERDANT GREEN
an Oxford Freshman

Young Mr. Verdant Green has tallied up eighteen years of unobjectionable existence at home with his sisters, comfortably insulated from the horrors of public school and the tyranny of sporting activities. But when Mr. Larkyns, local rector and Verdant's tutor, persuades Mr. Green Senior that his student is sorely in need of a little worldly experience, the callow Verdant is dispatched to Oxford for matriculation. As the innocent lamb embarks upon the odyssey of university life with characteristic trusting confidence, he finds himself gambolling into a den of wolves . . .

WITHDRAWN

Books by Cuthbert Bede
Published by Ulverscroft:

THE FURTHER ADVENTURES OF
MR. VERDANT GREEN
MR. VERDANT GREEN, MARRIED
AND DONE FOR

CUTHBERT BEDE

THE ADVENTURES OF MR. VERDANT GREEN

an Oxford Freshman

Complete and Unabridged

ULVERSCROFT
Leicester

First published in Great Britain in 1853

This Large Print Edition
published 2016

The moral right of the author has been asserted

A catalogue record for this book is available
from the British Library.

ISBN 978–1–4448–2685–2

Published by
F. A. Thorpe (Publishing)
Anstey, Leicestershire

Set by Words & Graphics Ltd.
Anstey, Leicestershire
Printed and bound in Great Britain by
T. J. International Ltd., Padstow, Cornwall

This book is printed on acid-free paper

Contents

1

Mr. Verdant Green's
Relatives and Antecedents

If you will refer to the unpublished volume of
Burke's Landed Gentry, and turn to letter G,
article 'GREEN,' you will see that the Verdant
Greens are a family of some respectability
and of considerable antiquity. We meet with
them as early as 1096, flocking to the
Crusades among the followers of Peter the
Hermit, when one of their number, Greene
surnamed the Witless, mortgaged his lands in
order to supply his poorer companions with
the sinews of war. The family estate, however,
appears to have been redeemed and greatly
increased by his great-grandson, Hugo de
Greene, but was again jeoparded in the year
1456, when Basil Greene, being commissioned by Henry the Sixth to enrich his
sovereign by discovering the philosopher's
stone, squandered the greater part of his
fortune in unavailing experiments; while his
son, who was also infected with the spirit of
the age, was blown up in his laboratory when
just on the point of discovering the elixir of

life. It seems to have been about this time that the Greenes became connected by marriage with the equally old family of the Verdants; and, in the year 1510, we find a Verdant Greene as justice of the peace for the county of Warwick, presiding at the trial of three decrepit old women, who, being found guilty of transforming themselves into cats, and in that shape attending the nightly assemblies of evil spirits, were very properly pronounced by him to be witches, and were burnt with all due solemnity.

In tracing the records of the family, we do not find that any of its members attained to great eminence in the state, either in the counsels of the senate or the active services of the field; or that they amassed any unusual amount of wealth or landed property. But we may perhaps ascribe these circumstances to the fact of finding the Greens, generation after generation, made the dupes of more astute minds, and when the hour of danger came, left to manage their own affairs in the best way they could, — a way that commonly ended in their mismanagement and total confusion. Indeed, the idiosyncrasy of the family appears to have been so well known, that we continually meet with them performing the character of catspaw to some monkey who had seen and understood much more of the world than they had, — putting their hands to the fire, and only finding out their mistake when they had burned their fingers.

In this way the family of the Verdant Greens never got beyond a certain point either in wealth or station, but were always the same unsuspicious, credulous, respectable, easy-going people in one century as another, with the same boundless confidence in their fellow-creatures, and the same readiness to oblige society by putting their names to little bills, merely for form's and friendship's sake. The Vavasour Verdant Green, with the slashed velvet doublet and point-lace fall, who (having a well-stocked purse) was among the favoured courtiers of the Merry Monarch, and who allowed that monarch in his merriness to borrow his purse, with the simple I.O.U. of 'Odd's fish! you shall take mine to-morrow!' and who never (of course) saw the sun rise on the day of repayment, was but the prototype of the Verdant Greens in the full-bottomed wigs, and buckles and shorts of George I.'s day, who were nearly beggared by the bursting of the Mississippi Scheme and South-Sea Bubble; and these, in their turn, were duly represented by their successors. And thus the family character was handed down with the family nose, until they both re-appeared (according to the veracious chronicle of Burke, to which we have referred), in

'VERDANT GREEN, of the Manor Green, Co. Warwick, Gent., who married Mary, only surviving child of Samuel Sappey, Esq., of Sapcot Hall, Co. Salop; by whom he has issue, one son, and three daughters: Mary,-VERDANT,-Helen,-Fanny.'

Mr. Burke is unfeeling enough to give the dates when this bunch of Greens first made their appearance in the world; but these dates we withhold, from a delicate regard to personal feelings, which will be duly appreciated by those who have felt the sacredness of their domestic hearth to be tampered with by the obtrusive impertinences of a census-paper.

It is sufficient for our purpose to say, that our hero, Mr. Verdant Green, junior, was born much in the same way as other folk. And although pronounced by Mrs. Toosypegs his nurse, when yet in the first crimson blush of his existence, to be 'a perfect progidy, mum, which I ought to be able to pronounce, 'avin nuss'd a many parties through their trouble, and being aweer of what is doo to a Hinfant,' — yet we are not aware that his *debut* on the stage of life, although thus applauded by such a *clacqueur* as the indiscriminating Toosypegs, was announced to the world at large by any other means than the notices in the county papers, and the six-shilling advertisement in the *Times*.

'Progidy' though he was, even as a baby, yet Mr. Verdant Green's nativity seems to have been chronicled merely in this everyday manner, and does not appear to have been accompanied by any of those more monstrous phenomena, which in earlier ages attended the production of a *genuine* prodigy. We are not aware that Mrs. Green's favourite Alderney spoke on that occasion, or conducted itself otherwise than as unaccustomed to public speaking as usual. Neither can we verify the assertion of the intelligent Mr. Mole the gardener, that the plaster Apollo in the Long Walk was observed to be bathed in a profuse perspiration, either from its feeling compelled to keep up the good old classical custom, or because the weather was damp. Neither are we bold enough to entertain an opinion that the chickens in the poultry-yard refused their customary food; or that the horses in the stable shook with trembling fear; or that any thing, or any body, saving and excepting Mrs. Toosypegs, betrayed any consciousness that a real and genuine prodigy had been given to the world.

However, during the first two years of his life, which were passed chiefly in drinking, crying, and sleeping, Mr. Verdant Green met with as much attention, and received as fair a share of approbation, as usually falls to the lot of the most favoured of infants. Then Mrs. Toosypegs again took up her position in the house, and his reign was over. Faithful to her mission, she pronounced the new baby to be *the* 'progidy,' and she was believed. But thus it is all through life; the new baby displaces the old; the second love supplants the first; we find fresh friends to shut out the memories of former ones; and in nearly everything we discover that there is a Number 2 which can put out of joint the nose of Number 1.

Once more the shadow of Mrs. Toosypegs fell upon the walls of Manor Green; and then, her mission being accomplished, she passed away for ever; and our hero was left to be the sole son and heir, and the prop and pride of the house of Green.

And if it be true that the external forms of nature exert a hidden but powerful sway over the dawning perceptions of the mind, and shape its thoughts to harmony with the things around, then most certainly ought Mr. Verdant Green to have been born a poet; for he grew up amid those scenes whose immortality is, that they inspired the soul of Shakespeare with his deathless fancies!

The Manor Green was situated in one of

the loveliest spots in all Warwickshire; a county so rich in all that constitutes the picturesqueness of a true English landscape. Looking from the drawing-room windows of the house, you saw in the near foreground the pretty French garden, with its fantastic parti-coloured beds, and its broad gravelled walks and terrace; proudly promenading which, or perched on the stone balustrade, might be seen perchance a peacock flaunting his beauties in the sun. Then came the carefully kept gardens, bounded on the one side by the Long Walk and a grove of shrubs and oaks; and on the other side by a double avenue of stately elms, that led, through velvet turf of brightest green, down past a little rustic lodge, to a gently sloping valley, where were white walls and rose-clustered gables of cottages peeping out from the embosoming trees, that betrayed the village beauties they seemed loth to hide. Then came the grey church-tower, dark with shrouding ivy; then another clump of stately elms, tenanted by cawing rooks; then a yellow stretch of bright meadow-land, dappled over with browsing kine knee-deep in grass and flowers; then a deep pool that mirrored all, and shone like silver; then more trees with floating shade, and homesteads rich in wheat-stacks; then a willowy brook that sparkled on merrily to an old mill-wheel, whose slippery stairs it lazily got down, and sank to quiet rest in the stream below; then came, crowding in rich profusion, wide-spreading woods and antlered oaks; and golden gorse and purple heather; and sunny orchards, with their dark-green waves that in Spring foamed white with blossoms; and then gently swelling hills that rose to close the scene and frame the picture.

Such was the view from the Manor Green. And full of inspiration as such a scene was, yet Mr. Verdant Green never accomplished (as far as poetical inspiration was concerned) more than an 'Address to the Moon,' which he could just as well have written in any other part of the country, and which, commencing with the noble aspiration,

'O moon, that shinest in the heaven so
   blue,
I only wish that I could shine like you!'

and terminating with one of those fine touches of nature which rise superior to the trammels of ordinary versification,

'But I to bed must be going soon,
So I will not address thee more,
   O moon!'

will no doubt go down to posterity in the Album of his sister Mary.

For the first fourteen years of his life, the education of Mr. Verdant Green was conducted wholly under the shadow of his paternal roof, upon principles fondly imagined to be the soundest and purest for the formation of his character. Mrs. Green, who was as good and motherly a soul as ever lived, was yet (as we have shewn) one of the Sappeys of Sapcot, a family that were not renowned either for common sense or worldly wisdom, and her notions of a boy's education were of that kind laid down by her favourite poet, Cowper, in his 'Tirocinium' that we are

'Well-tutor's *only* while we share
A mother's lectures and a nurse's care;'

and in her horror of all other kind of instruction (not that she admitted Mrs. Toosypegs to her counsels), she fondly kept Master Verdant at her own apron-strings. The task of teaching his young idea how to shoot was committed chiefly to his sisters' governess, and he regularly took his place with them in the school-room. These daily exercises and mental drillings were subject to the inspection of their maiden-aunt, Miss

9

Virginia Verdant, a first cousin of Mr. Green's, who had come to visit at the Manor during Master Verdant's infancy, and had remained there ever since; and this generalship was crowned with such success, that her nephew grew up the girlish companion of his sisters, with no knowledge of boyish sports, and no desire for them.

The motherly and spinsterial views regarding his education were favoured by the fact that he had no playmates of his own sex and age; and since his father was an only child, and his mother's brothers had died in their infancy, there were no cousins to initiate him into the mysteries of boyish games and feelings. Mr. Green was a man who only cared to live a quiet, easy-going life, and would have troubled himself but little about his neighbours, if he had had any; but the Manor Green lay in an agricultural district, and, saving the Rectory, there was no other large house for miles around. The rector's wife, Mrs. Larkyns, had died shortly after the birth of her first child, a son, who was being educated at a public school; and this was enough, in Mrs. Green's eyes, to make a too intimate acquaintance between her boy and Master Larkyns a thing by no means to be desired. With her favourite poet she would say,

'For public schools, 'tis public folly
    feeds;'

and, regarding them as the very hotbeds of all
that is wrong, she would turn a deaf, though
polite, ear to the rector whenever he said,
'Why don't you let your Verdant go with my
Charley? Charley is three years older than
Verdant, and would take him under his wing.'
Mrs. Green would as soon think of putting
one of her chickens under the wing of a hawk,
as intrusting the innocent Verdant to the care
of the scape-grace Charley; so she still
persisted in her own system of education,
despite all that the rector could advise to the
contrary.

As for Master Verdant, he was only too glad
at his mother's decision, for he partook of all
her alarm about public schools, though from
a different cause. It was not very often that he
visited at the Rectory during Master Charley's holidays; but when he did, that young
gentleman favoured him with such accounts
of the peculiar knack the second master
possessed of finding out all your tenderest
places when he 'licked a feller' for a false
quantity, that, 'by Jove! you couldn't sit down
for a fortnight without squeaking;' and of the
jolly mills they used to have with the town
cads, who would lie in wait for you, and half

11

kill you if they caught you alone; and of the fun it was to make a junior form fag for you, and do all your dirty work; — that Master Verdant's hair would almost stand on end at such horrors, and he would gasp for very dread lest such should ever be *his* dreadful doom.

And then Master Charley would take a malicious pleasure in consoling him, by saying, 'Of course, you know, you'll only have to fag for the first two or three years; then — if you get into the fourth form — you'll be able to have a fag for yourself. And it's awful fun, I can tell you, to see the way some of the fags get riled at cricket! You get a feller to give you a few balls, just for practice, and you hit the ball into another feller's ground; and then you tell your fag to go and pick it up. So he goes to do it, when the other feller sings out, 'Don't touch that ball, or I'll lick you!' So you tell the fag to come to you, and you say, 'Why don't you do as I tell you?' And he says, 'Please, sir!' and then the little beggar blubbers. So you say to him, 'None of that, sir! Touch your toes!' We always make 'em wear straps on purpose. And then his trousers go tight and beautiful, and you take out your strap and warm him! And then he goes to get the ball, and the other feller sings out, 'I told you to let that ball alone! Come here, sir!

Touch your toes!' So he warms him too; and then we go on all jolly. It's awful fun, I can tell you!'

Master Verdant would think it awful indeed; and, by his own fireside, would recount the deeds of horror to his trembling mother and sisters, whose imagination shuddered at the scenes from which they hoped their darling would be preserved.

Perhaps Master Charley had his own reasons for making matters worse than they really were; but, as long as the information he derived concerning public schools was of this description, so long did Master Verdant Green feel thankful at being kept away from them. He had a secret dread, too, of his friend's superior age and knowledge; and in his presence felt a bashful awe that made him glad to get back from the Rectory to his own sisters; while Master Charley, on the other hand, entertained a lad's contempt for one that could not fire off a gun, or drive a cricket-ball, or jump a ditch without falling into it. So the Rectory and the Manor Green lads saw but very little of each other; and, while the one went through his public-school course, the other was brought up at the women's apron-strings.

But though thus put under petticoat government, Mr. Verdant Green was not altogether freed from those tyrants of youth — the dead languages. His aunt Virginia was as learned a Blue as her esteemed ancestress in the court of Elizabeth, the very Virgin Queen of Blues; and under her guidance Master Verdant was dragged with painful diligence through the first steps of the road that was to take him to Parnassus. It was a great sight to see her sitting stiff and straight; — with her wonderfully undeceptive 'false front' of (somebody else's) black hair, graced on either side by four sausage-looking curls — as, with spectacles on nose and dictionary in hand, she instructed her nephew in those ingenuous arts which should soften his manners, and not permit him to be brutal. And, when they together entered upon the romantic page of Virgil (which was the extent of her classical reading), nothing would delight her more than to declaim their sonorous Arma-virumque-cano lines, where the intrinsic qualities of the verse surpassed the quantities that she gave to them.

Fain would Miss Virginia have made Virgil the end and aim of an educational existence, and so have kept her pupil entirely under her own care; but, alas! she knew nothing further; she had no acquaintance with Greek, and she had never flirted with Euclid; and the rector persuaded Mr. Green that these were indispensable to a boy's education. So, when Mr. Verdant Green was (in stable language) 'rising' sixteen, he went thrice a week to the Rectory, where Mr. Larkyns bestowed upon him a couple of hours, and taught him to conjugate {tupto}, and get over the *Pons Asinorum*. Mr. Larkyns found his pupil not a particularly brilliant scholar, but he was a plodding one; and though he learned slowly, yet the little he did learn was learned well.

Thus the Rectory and the home studies went hand and hand, and continued so, with but little interruption, for more than two years; and Mr. Verdant Green had for some time assumed the *toga virilis* of stick-up collars and swallow-tail coats, that so effectually cut us off from the age of innocence; and the small family festival that annually celebrated his birthday had just been held for the eighteenth time, when

'A change came o'er the spirit of *his* dream.'

2

Mr. Verdant Green
is to be an Oxford Freshman

One day when the family at the Manor Green had assembled for luncheon, the rector was announced. He came in and joined them, saying, with his usual friendly *bonhomie*, 'A very well-timed visit, I think! Your bell rang out its summons as I came up the avenue. Mrs. Green, I've gone through the formality of looking over the accounts of your clothing-club, and, as usual, I find them correctness itself; and here is my subscription for the next year. Miss Green, I hope that you have not forgotten the lesson in logic that Tommy Jones gave you yesterday afternoon?'

'Oh, what was that?' cried her two sisters; who took it in turns with her to go for a short time in every day to the village-school which their father and the rector had established: 'Pray tell us, Mr. Larkyns! Mary has said nothing about it.'

'Then,' replied the rector, 'I am tongue-tied, until I have my fair friend's permission to reveal how the teacher was taught.'

Mary shook her sunny ringlets, and laughingly gave him the required permission.

'You must know, then,' said Mr. Larkyns, 'that Miss Mary was giving one of those delightful object-lessons, wherein she blends so much instructive.'

'I'll trouble you for the butter, Mr. Larkyns,' interrupted Mary, rather maliciously.

The rector was grey-headed, and a privileged friend. 'My dear,' he said, 'I was just giving it you. However, the object-lesson was going on; the subject being *Quadrupeds*, which Miss Mary very properly explained to be 'things with four legs.' Presently, she said to her class, 'Tell me the names of some quadrupeds?' when Tommy Jones, thrusting out his hand with the full conviction that he was making an important suggestion, exclaimed, 'Chairs and tables!' That was turning the tables upon Miss Mary with a vengeance!'

During luncheon the conversation glided into a favourite theme with Mrs. Green and Miss Virginia, — Verdant's studies: when Mr. Larkyns, after some good-natured praise of his diligence, said, 'By the way, Green, he's now quite old enough, and prepared enough for matriculation: and I suppose you are thinking of it.'

Mr. Green was thinking of no such thing.

He had never been at college himself, and had never heard of his father having been there; and having the old-fashioned, what-was-good-enough-for-my-father-is-good-enough-for-me sort of feeling, it had never occurred to him that his son should be brought up otherwise than he himself had been. The setting-out of Charles Larkyns for college, two years before, had suggested no other thought to Mr. Green's mind, than that a university was the natural sequence of a public school; and since Verdant had not been through the career of the one, he deemed him to be exempt from the other.

The motherly ears of Mrs. Green had been caught by the word 'matriculation,' a phrase quite unknown to her; and she said, 'If it's vaccination that you mean, Mr. Larkyns, my dear Verdant was done only last year, when we thought the small-pox was about; so I think he's quite safe.'

Mr. Larkyns' politeness was sorely tried to restrain himself from giving vent to his feelings in a loud burst of laughter; but Mary gallantly came to his relief by saying, 'Matriculation means, being entered at a university. Don't you remember, dearest mamma, when Mr. Charles Larkyns went up to Oxford to be matriculated last January two years?'

'Ah, yes! I do now. But I wish I had your memory, my dear.'

And Mary blushed, and flattered herself that she succeeded in looking as though Mr. Charles Larkyns and his movements were objects of perfect indifference to her.

So, after luncheon, Mr. Green and the rector paced up and down the long-walk, and talked the matter over. The burden of Mr. Green's discourse was this: 'You see, sir, I don't intend my boy to go into the Church, like yours; but, when anything happens to me, he'll come into the estate, and have to settle down as the squire of the parish. So I don't exactly see what would be the use of sending him to a university, where, I dare say, he'd spend a good deal of money, — not that I should grudge that, though; — and perhaps not be quite such a good lad as he's always been to me, sir. And, by George! (I beg your pardon,) I think his mother would break her heart to lose him; and I don't know what we should do without him, as he's never been away from us a day, and his sisters would miss him. And he's not a lad, like your Charley, that could fight his way in the world, and I don't think he'd be altogether happy. And as he's not got to depend upon his talents for his bread and cheese, the knowledge he's got at home, and from you, sir, seems to me quite enough to carry him through life. So, altogether, I think Verdant will do very well as he is, and perhaps we'd better say no more about the matriculation.'

But the rector *would* say more; and he expressed his mind thus: 'It is not so much from what Verdant would learn in Latin and Greek, and such things as make up a part of the education, that I advise your sending him to a university; but more from what he would gain by mixing with a large body of young men of his own age, who represent the best classes of a mixed society, and who may justly be taken as fair samples of its feelings and talents. It is formation of character that I regard as one of the greatest of the many great ends of a university system; and if for this reason alone, I should advise you to send your future country squire to college. Where else will he be able to meet with so great a number of those of his own class, with whom he will have to mix in the after changes of life, and for whose feelings and tone a college-course will give him the proper key-note? Where else can he learn so quickly in three years, what other men will perhaps be striving for through life, without attaining, — that self-reliance which will enable him to mix at ease in any society, and to feel the equal of its members? And, besides all this, — and each of these points in the education of a young man is, to my mind, a strong one, — where else could he be more completely 'under tutors and governors,' and more thoroughly under *surveillance*, than in a place where college-laws are no respecters of persons, and seek to keep the wild blood of youth within its due bounds? There is something in the very atmosphere of a university that seems to engender refined thoughts and noble feelings; and lamentable indeed must be the state of any young man who can pass through the three years of his college residence, and bring away no higher aims, no worthier purposes, no better thoughts, from all the holy associations which have been crowded around him. Such advantages as these are not to be regarded with indifference; and though they come in secondary ways, and possess the mind almost imperceptibly, yet they are of primary importance in the formation of character, and may mould it into the more perfect man. And as long as I had the power, I would no more think of depriving a child of mine of such good means towards a good end, than I would of keeping him from any thing else that was likely to improve his mind or affect his heart.'

Mr. Larkyns put matters in a new light; and Mr. Green began to think that a university career might be looked at from more than one point of view. But as old prejudices are not so easily overthrown as the lath-and-plaster erections of mere newly-formed opinion, Mr. Green was not yet won over by Mr. Larkyns' arguments. 'There was my father,' he said, 'who was one of the worthiest and kindest men living; and I believe he never went to college, nor did he think it necessary that I should go; and I trust I'm no worse a man than my father.'

'Ah! Green,' replied the rector; 'the old argument! But you must not judge the present age by the past; nor measure out to *your* son the same degree of education that your father might think sufficient for *you*. When you and I were boys, Green, these things were thought of very differently to what they are in the present day; and when your father gave you a respectable education at a classical school, he did all that he thought was requisite to form you into a country gentleman, and fit you for that station in life you were destined to fill. But consider what a progressive age it is that we live in; and you will see that the standard of education has been considerably raised since the days when you and I did the 'propria quae maribus' together; and that when he comes to mix in society, more will be demanded of the son than was expected from the father. And besides this, think in how many ways it will benefit Verdant to send him to college. By mixing more in the world, and being called upon to act and think for himself, he will gradually gain that experience, without which a man cannot arm himself to meet the difficulties that beset all of us, more or less, in the battle of life. He is just of an age, when some change from the narrowed circle of home is necessary. God forbid that I should ever speak in any but the highest terms of the moral good it must do every young man to live under his mother's watchful eye, and be ever in the company of pure-minded sisters. Indeed I feel this more perhaps than many other parents would, because my lad, from his earliest years, has been deprived of such tender training, and cut off from such sweet society. But yet, with all this high regard for such home influences, I put it to you, if there will not grow up in the boy's mind, when he begins to draw near to man's estate, a very weariness of all this, from its very sameness; a surfeiting, as it were, of all these delicacies, and a longing for something to break the monotony of what will gradually become to him a humdrum horse-in-the-mill kind of country life? And it is just at this critical time that college life steps in to his aid. With his new life a new light bursts upon his mind; he finds that he is not the little household-god he had fancied himself to be; his word is no longer the law of the Medes and Persians, as it was at home; he meets with none of those little flatteries from partial relatives, or fawning servants, that were growing into a part of his existence; but he has to bear contradiction and reproof, to find himself only an equal with others, when he can gain that equality by his own deserts; and, in short, he daily progresses in that knowledge of himself, which, from the *gnothiseauton* days down to our own, has been found to be about the most useful of all knowledge; for it gives a man stability of character, and braces up his mental energies to a healthy enjoyment of the business of life. And so, Green, I would advise you, above all things, to let Verdant go to college.'

Much more did the rector say, not only on this occasion, but on others; and the more frequently he returned to the charge, the less resistance were his arguments met with; and the result was, that Mr. Green was fully persuaded that a university was the proper sphere for his son to move in. But it was not without many a pang and much secret misgiving that Mrs. Green would consent to suffer her beloved Verdant to run the risk of those dreadful contaminations which she imagined would inevitably accompany every college career. Indeed, she thought it an act of the greatest heroism (or, if you object to the word, heroineism) to be won over to say 'yes' to the proposal; and it was not until Miss Virginia had recited to her the deeds of all the mothers of Greece and Rome who had suffered for their children's sake, that Mrs. Green would consent to sacrifice her maternal feelings at the sacred altar of duty.

When the point had been duly settled, that Mr. Verdant Green was to receive a university education, the next question to be decided was, to which of the three Universities should he go? To Oxford, Cambridge, or Durham? But this was a matter which was soon determined upon. Mr. Green at once put Durham aside, on account of its infancy, and its wanting the *prestige* that attaches to the names of the two great Universities. Cambridge was treated quite as summarily, because Mr. Green had conceived the notion that nothing but mathematics were ever thought or talked of there; and as he himself had always had an abhorrence of them from his youth up, when he was hebdomadally flogged for not getting-up his weekly propositions, he thought that his son should be spared some of the personal disagreeables that he himself had encountered; for Mr. Green remembered to have heard that the great Newton was horsed during the time that he was a Cambridge undergraduate, and he had a hazy idea that the same indignities were still practised there.

But the circumstance that chiefly decided Mr. Green to choose Oxford as the arena for Verdant's performances was, that he would have a companion, and, as he hoped, a mentor, in the rector's son, Mr. Charles Larkyns, who would not only be able to cheer him on his first entrance, but also would introduce him to select and quiet friends, put him in the way of lectures, and initiate him into all the mysteries of the place; all which the rector professed his son would be glad to do, and would be delighted to see his old friend and playfellow within the classic walls of Alma Mater.

Oxford having been selected for the university, the next point to be decided was the college.

'You cannot,' said the rector, 'find a much better college than Brazenface, where my lad is. It always stands well in the class-list, and keeps a good name with its tutors. There are a nice gentlemanly set of men there; and I am proud to say, that my lad would be able to introduce Verdant to some of the best. This will of course be much to his advantage. And besides this, I am on very intimate terms with Dr. Portman, the master of the college; and, if they should not happen to be very full, no doubt I could get Verdant admitted at once. This too will be of advantage to him; for I can tell you that there are secrets in all these matters, and that at many colleges that I could name, unless you knew the principal, or had some introduction or other potent spell to work with, your son's name would have to remain on the books two or three years before he could be entered; and this, at Verdant's age, would be a serious objection. At one or two of the colleges indeed this is almost necessary, under any circumstances, on account of the great number of applicants; but at Brazenface there is not this over-crowding; and I have no doubt, if I write to Dr. Portman, but what I can get rooms for Verdant without much loss of time.'

'Brazenface be it then!' said Mr. Green, 'and I am sure that Verdant will enter there with very many advantages; and the sooner the better, so that he may be the longer with Mr. Charles. But when must his — his what-d'ye-call-it, come off?'

'His matriculation?' replied the rector.

27

'Why although it is not usual for men to commence residence at the time of their matriculation, still it is sometimes done. And as my lad will, if all goes on well, be leaving Oxford next year, perhaps it would be better, on that account, that Verdant should enter upon his residence as soon as he has matriculated.'

Mr. Green thought so too; and Verdant, upon being appealed to, had no objection to this course, or, indeed, to any other that was decided to be necessary for him; though it must be confessed, that he secretly shared somewhat of his mother's feelings as he looked forward into the blank and uncertain prospect of his college life. Like a good and dutiful son, however, his father's wishes were law; and he no more thought of opposing them, than he did of discovering the north pole, or paying off the national debt.

So all this being duly settled, and Mrs. Green being entirely won over to the proceeding, the rector at once wrote to Dr. Portman, and in due time received a reply to the effect, that they were very full at Brazenface, but that luckily there was one set of rooms which would be vacant at the commencement of the Easter term; at which time he should be very glad to see the gentleman his friend spoke of.

3

Mr. Verdant Green Leaves
the Home of his Ancestors

The time till Easter passed very quickly, for much had to be done in it. Verdant read up most desperately for his matriculation, associating that initiatory examination with the most dismal visions of plucking, and other college tortures.

His mother was laying in for him a new stock of linen, sufficient in quantity to provide him for years of emigration; while his father was busying himself about the plate that it was requisite to take, buying it bran-new, and of the most solid silver, and having it splendidly engraved with the family crest, and the motto 'Semper virens.'

Infatuated Mr. Green! If you could have foreseen that those spoons and forks would have soon passed, — by a mysterious system of loss which undergraduate powers can never fathom, — into the property of Mr. Robert Filcher, the excellent, though occasionally erratic, scout of your beloved son, and from thence have melted, not 'into thin air,' but into a residuum whose mass might be expressed by the equivalent of coins of a thin and golden description, — if you could but have foreseen this, then, infatuated but affectionate parent, you would have been content to have let your son and heir represent the ancestral wealth by mere electro-plate, albata, or any sham that would equally well have served his purpose!

As for Miss Virginia Verdant, and the other woman portion of the Green community, they fully occupied their time until the day of separation came, by elaborating articles of feminine workmanship, as *souvenirs*, by which dear Verdant might, in the land of the strangers, recall visions of home. These were presented to him with all due state on the morning of the day previous to that on which he was to leave the home of his ancestors.

All the articles were useful as well as ornamental. There was a purse from Helen, which, besides being a triumph of art in the way of bead decoration, was also, it must be allowed, a very useful present, unless one happened to carry one's riches in a *portemonnaie*. There was a pair of braces from Mary, worked with an ecclesiastical pattern of a severe character — very appropriate for academical wear, and extremely effective for all occasions when the coat had to be taken off in public. And there was a watch-pocket from Fanny, to hang over Verdant's night-capped head, and serve as a depository for the golden mechanical turnip that had been handed down in the family, as a watch, for the last three generations. And there was a pair of woollen comforters knit by Miss Virginia's own fair hands; and there were other woollen articles of domestic use, which were contributed by Mrs. Green for her son's personal comfort. To these, Miss Virginia thoughtfully added an infallible recipe for the toothache, — an infliction to which she was a martyr, and for the general relief of which in others, she constituted herself a species of toothache missionary; for, as she said, 'You might, my dear Verdant, be seized with that painful disease, and not have me by your side to cure it'; which it was very probable he would not, if college rules were strictly carried out at Brazenface.

All these articles were presented to Mr. Verdant Green with many speeches and great ceremony; while Mr. Green stood by, and smiled benignantly upon the scene, and his son beamed through his glasses (which his defective sight obliged him constantly to wear) with the most serene aspect.

It was altogether a great day of preparation,

and one which it was well for the constitution of the household did not happen very often; for the house was reduced to that summerset condition usually known in domestic parlance as 'upside down.' Mr. Verdant Green personally superintended the packing of his goods; a performance which was only effected by the united strength of the establishment. Butler, Footman, Coachman, Lady's-maid, Housemaid, and Buttons were all pressed into the service; and the coachman, being a man of some weight, was found to be of great use in effecting a junction of the locks and hasps of over-filled book-boxes. It was astonishing to see all the amount of literature that Mr. Verdant Green was about to convey to the seat of learning: there was enough to stock a small Bodleian. As the owner stood, with his hands behind him, placidly surveying the scene of preparation, a meditative spectator might have possibly compared him to the hero of the engraving 'Moses going to the fair,' that was then hanging just over his head; for no one could have set out for the great Oxford booth of this Vanity Fair with more simplicity and trusting confidence than Mr. Verdant Green.

When the trunks had at last been packed, they were then, by the thoughtful suggestion of Miss Virginia, provided each with a canvas covering, after the manner of the luggage of females, and labelled with large direction-cards filled with the most ample particulars concerning their owner and his destination.

It had been decided that Mr. Verdant Green, instead of reaching Oxford by rail, should make his *entree* behind the four horses that drew the Birmingham and Oxford coach; — one of the few four-horse coaches that still ran for any distance; and which, as the more pleasant means of conveyance, was generally patronized by Mr. Charles Larkyns in preference to the rail; for the coach passed within three miles of the Manor Green, whereas the nearest railway was at a much greater distance, and could not be so conveniently reached. Mr. Green had determined upon accompanying Verdant to Oxford, that he might have the satisfaction of seeing him safely landed there, and might also himself form an acquaintance with a city of which he had heard so much, and which would be doubly interesting to him now that his son was enrolled a member of its University. Their seats had been secured a fortnight previous; for the rector had told Mr. Green that so many men went up by the coach, that unless he made an early application, he would altogether fail in obtaining places; so a letter had been dispatched to 'the Swan' coach-office at Birmingham, from which place the coach started, and two outside seats had been put at Mr. Green's disposal.

The day at length arrived, when Mr. Verdant Green for the first time in his life (on any important occasion) was to leave the paternal roof; and it must be confessed that it was a proceeding which caused him some anxiety, and that he was not sorry when the carriage was at the door to bear him away, before (shall it be confessed?) his tears had got the mastery over him.

As it was, by the judicious help of his sisters, he passed the Rubicon in courageous style, and went through the form of breakfast with the greatest hilarity, although with several narrow escapes of suffocation from choking. The thought that he was going to be an Oxford MAN fortunately assisted him in the preservation of that tranquil dignity and careless ease which he considered to be the necessary adjuncts of the manly character, more especially as developed in that peculiar biped he was about to be transformed into; and Mr. Verdant Green was enabled to say 'Good-bye' with a firm voice and undimmed spectacles.

All crowded to the door to have a last shake of the hand; the maid-servants peeped from the upper windows; and Miss Virginia sobbed out a blessing, which was rendered of a striking and original character by being mixed up with instructions never to forget what she had taught him in his Latin grammar, and always to be careful to guard against the toothache. And amid the good-byes and write-oftens that usually accompany a departure, the carriage rolled down the avenue to the lodge, where was Mr. Mole the gardener, and also Mrs. Mole, and, moreover, the Mole olive-branches, all gathered at the open gate to say farewell to the young master. And just as they were about to mount the hill leading out of the village, who should be there but the rector lying in wait for them and ready to walk up the hill by their side, and say a few kindly words at parting. Well might Mr. Verdant Green begin to regard himself as the topic of the village, and think that going to Oxford was really an affair of some importance.

They were in good time for the coach; and the ringing notes of the guard's bugle made them aware of its approach some time before they saw it rattling merrily along in its cloud of dust. What a sight it was when it did come near! The cloud that had enveloped it was discovered to be not dust only, but smoke from the cigars, meerschaums, and short clay pipes of a full complement of gentlemen passengers, scarcely one of whom seemed to have passed his twentieth year. No bonnet betokening a female traveller could be seen either inside or out; and that lady was indeed lucky who escaped being an inside passenger on the following day. Nothing but a lapse of time, or the complete re-lining of the coach, could purify it from the attacks of the four gentlemen who were now doing their best to convert it into a divan; and the consumption of tobacco on that day between Birmingham and Oxford must have materially benefited the revenue. The passengers were not limited to the two-legged ones, there were four-footed ones also. Sporting dogs, fancy dogs, ugly dogs, rat-killing dogs, short-haired dogs, long-haired dogs, dogs like muffs, dogs like mops, dogs of all colours and of all breeds and sizes, appeared thrusting out their black noses from all parts of the coach. Portmanteaus were piled upon the roof; gun-boxes peeped out suspiciously here and there; bundles of sticks, canes, foils, fishing-rods, and whips, appeared strapped together in every direction; while all round about the coach,

'Like a swarth Indian with his belt of
  beads,'

hat-boxes dangled in leathery profusion. The

Oxford coach on an occasion like this was a sight to be remembered.

A 'Wo-ho-ho, my beauties!' brought the smoking wheelers upon their haunches; and Jehu, saluting with his elbow and whip finger, called out in the husky voice peculiar to a dram-drinker, 'Are you the two houtside gents for Hoxfut?' To which Mr. Green replied in the affirmative; and while the luggage (the canvas-covered, ladylike look of which was such a contrast to that of the other passengers) was being quickly transferred to the coach-top, he and Verdant ascended to the places reserved for them behind the coachman. Mr. Green saw at a glance that all the passengers were Oxford men, dressed in every variety of Oxford fashion, and exhibiting a pleasing diversity of Oxford manners. Their private remarks on the two new-comers were, like stage 'asides,' perfectly audible.

'Decided case of governor!' said one.

'Undoubted ditto of freshman!' observed another.

'Looks ferociously mild in his gig-lamps!' remarked a third, alluding to Mr. Verdant Green's spectacles.

'And jolly green all over!' wound up a fourth.

Mr. Green, hearing his name (as he

thought) mentioned, turned to the small young gentleman who had spoken, and politely said, 'Yes, my name is Green; but you have the advantage of me, sir.'

'Oh! have I?' replied the young gentleman in the most affable manner, and not in the least disconcerted; 'my name's Bouncer: I remember seeing you when I was a babby. How's the old woman?' And without waiting to hear Mr. Green loftily reply, 'Mrs. Green — my WIFE, sir — is quite well — and I do NOT remember to have seen you, or ever heard your name, sir!' — little Mr. Bouncer made some most unearthly noises on a post-horn as tall as himself, which he had brought for the delectation of himself and his friends, and the alarm of every village they passed through.

'Never mind the dog, sir,' said the gentleman who sat between Mr. Bouncer and Mr. Green; 'he won't hurt you. It's only his play; he always takes notice of strangers.'

'But he is tearing my trousers,' expostulated Mr. Green, who was by no means partial to the 'play' of a thoroughbred terrier.

'Ah! he's an uncommon sensible dog,' observed his master; 'he's always on the look-out for rats everywhere. It's the Wellington boots that does it; he's accustomed to have a rat put into a boot, and he worries it out how he can. I daresay he thinks you've got one in yours.'

'But I've got nothing of the sort, sir; I must request you to keep your dog — ' A violent fit of coughing, caused by a well-directed volley of smoke from his neighbour's lips, put a stop to Mr. Green's expostulations.

'I hope my weed is no annoyance?' said the gentleman; 'if it is, I will throw it away.'

To which piece of politeness Mr. Green could, of course, only reply, between fits of coughing, 'Not in the least I — assure you, — I am very fond — of tobacco — in the open air.'

'Then I daresay you'll do as we are doing, and smoke a weed yourself,' said the gentleman, as he offered Mr. Green a plethoric cigar-case. But Mr. Green's expression of approbation regarding tobacco was simply theoretical; so he treated his neighbour's offer as magazine editors do the MSS. of unknown contributors — it was 'declined with thanks.'

Mr. Verdant Green had already had to make a similar reply to a like proposal on the part of his left-hand neighbour, who was now expressing violent admiration for our hero's top-coat.

'Ain't that a good style of coat, Charley?' he observed to his neighbour. 'I wish I'd seen it before I got this over-coat! There's something sensible about a real, unadulterated top-coat; and there's a style in the way in which they've let down the skirts, and put on the velvet collar and cuffs regardless of expense, that really quite goes to one's heart. Now I daresay the man that built that,' he said, more particularly addressing the owner of the coat, 'condescends to live in a village, and waste his sweetness on the desert air, while a noble field might be found for his talent in a University town. That coat will make quite a sensation in Oxford. Won't it, Charley?'

And when Charley, quoting a popular actor (totally unknown to our hero), said, 'I believe you, my bo-oy!' Mr. Verdant Green began to feel quite proud of the abilities of their village tailor, and thought what two delightful companions he had met with. The rest of the journey further cemented (as he thought) their friendship; so that he was fairly astonished, when on meeting them the next day, they stared him full in the face, and passed on without taking any more notice of him. But freshmen cannot learn the mysteries of college etiquette in a day.

However, we are anticipating. They had not yet got to Oxford, though, from the pace at which they were going, it appeared as if they would soon reach there; for the coachman had given up his seat and the reins to the box-passenger, who appeared to be as used to the business as the coachman himself; and he was now driving them, not only in a most scientific manner, but also at a great pace. Mr. Green was not particularly pleased with the change in the four-wheeled government; but when they went down the hill at a quick trot, the heavy luggage making the coach rock to and fro with the speed, his fears increased painfully. They culminated, as the trot increased into a canter, and then broke into a gallop as they swept along the level road at the bottom of the hill, and rattled up the rise of another. As the horses walked over the brow of the hill, with smoking flanks and jingling harness, Mr. Green recovered sufficient breath to expostulate with the coachman for suffering — 'a mere lad,' he was about to say but fortunately checked himself in time, — for suffering any one else than the regular driver to have the charge of the coach.

'You never fret yourself about that, sir,' replied the man; 'I knows my bis'ness, as well as my dooties to self and purprietors, and I'd never go for to give up the ribbins to any party but wot had shewed hisself fitted to 'andle 'em. And I think I may say this for the genelman as has got 'em now, that he's fit to be fust vip to the Queen herself; and I'm proud to call him my poople. Why, sir, — if his honour here will pardon me for makin' so free, — this 'ere gent is Four-in-hand Fosbrooke, of which you *must* have heerd on.'

Mr. Green replied that he had not had that pleasure.

'Ah! a pleasure you *may* call it, sir, with parfect truth,' replied the coachman; 'but, lor bless me, sir, weer *can* you have lived?'

The 'poople' who had listened to this, highly amused, slightly turned his head, and said to Mr. Green, 'Pray don't feel any alarm, sir; I believe you are quite safe under my guidance. This is not the first time by many that I have driven this coach — not to mention others; and you may conclude that I should not have gained the *sobriquet* to which my worthy friend has alluded without having *some* pretensions to a knowledge of the art of driving.'

Mr. Green murmured his apologies for his mistrust, — expressed perfect faith in Mr. Fosbrooke's skill — and then lapsed into silent meditation on the various arts and sciences in which the gentlemen of the University of Oxford seemed to be most proficient, and pictured to himself what would be his feelings if he ever came to see

Verdant driving a coach! There certainly did not appear to be much probability of such an event; but can any *pater familias* say what even the most carefully brought up young Hopeful will do when he has arrived at years of indiscretion?

Altogether, Mr. Green did not particularly enjoy the journey. Besides the dogs and cigars, which to him were equal nuisances, little Mr. Bouncer was perpetually producing unpleasant post-horn effects, — which he called 'sounding his octaves,' — and destroying the effect of the airs on the guard's key-bugle, by joining in them at improper times and with discordant measures. Mr. Green, too, could not but perceive that the majority of the conversation that was addressed to himself and his son (though more particularly to the latter), although couched in politest form, was yet of a tendency calculated to 'draw them out' for the amusement of their fellow-passengers. He also observed that the young gentlemen severally exhibited great capacity for the beer of Bass and the porter of Guinness, and were not averse even to liquids of a more spirituous description. Moreover, Mr. Green remarked that the ministering Hebes were invariably addressed by their Christian names, and were

43

familiarly conversed with as old acquaintances; most of them receiving direct offers of marriage or the option of putting up the banns on any Sunday in the middle of the week; while the inquiries after their grandmothers and the various members of their family circles were both numerous and gratifying. In all these verbal encounters little Mr. Bouncer particularly distinguished himself.

Woodstock was reached: 'Four-in-hand Fosbrooke' gave up the reins to the professional Jehu; and at last the towers, spires, and domes of Oxford appeared in sight. The first view of the City of Colleges is always one that will be long remembered. Even the railway traveller, who enters by the least imposing approach, and can scarcely see that he is in Oxford before he has reached Folly Bridge, must yet regard the city with mingled feelings of delight and surprise as he looks across the Christ Church meadows and rolls past the Tom Tower. But he who approaches Oxford from the Henley Road, and looks upon that unsurpassed prospect from Magdalen Bridge, — or he who enters the city, as Mr. Green did, from the Woodstock Road, and rolls down the shady avenue of St. Giles', between St. John's College and the Taylor Buildings, and past the graceful Martyrs' Memorial, will receive impressions such as probably no other city in the world could convey.

As the coach clattered down the Corn-market, and turned the corner by Carfax into High Street, Mr. Bouncer, having been compelled in deference to University scruples to lay aside his post-horn, was consoling himself by chanting the following words, selected probably in compliment to Mr. Verdant Green.

'To Oxford, a Freshman so modest,
I enter'd one morning in March;
And the figure I cut was the oddest,
All spectacles, choker, and starch.
   Whack fol lol, lol iddity, &c.

From the top of 'the Royal Defiance,'
Jack Adams, who coaches so well,
Set me down in the regions of science,
In front of the Mire Hotel.
   Whack fol lol, lol iddity, &c.

'Sure never man's prospects were
  brighter,'
I said, as I jumped from my perch;
'So quickly arrived at the Mitre,
Oh, I'm sure to get on in the Church!'
   Whack fol lol, lol iddity, &c.'

By the time Mr. Bouncer finished these words, the coach appropriately drew up at the 'Mitre,' and the passengers tumbled off amid a knot of gownsmen collected on the pavement to receive them. But no sooner were Mr. Green and our hero set down, than they were attacked by a horde of the aborigines of Oxford, who, knowing by vulture-like sagacity the aspect of a freshman and his governor, swooped down upon them in the guise of impromptu porters, and made an indiscriminate attack upon the luggage. It was only by the display of the greatest presence of mind that Mr. Verdant Green recovered his effects, and prevented his canvas-covered boxes from being carried off in the wheel-barrows that were trundling off in all directions to the various colleges.

But at last all were safely secured. And soon, when a snug dinner had been discussed in a quiet room, and a bottle of the famous (though I have heard some call it 'infamous') Oxford port had been produced, Mr. Green, under its kindly influence, opened his heart to his son, and gave him much advice as to his forthcoming University career; being, of course, well calculated to do this from his intimate acquaintance with the subject.

Whether it was the extra glass of port, or whether it was the nature of his father's discourse, or whether it was the novelty of his situation, or whether it was all these circumstances combined, yet certain it was that Mr. Verdant Green's first night in Oxford was distinguished by a series, or rather confusion, of most remarkable dreams, in which bishops, archbishops, and hobgoblins elbowed one another for precedence; a beneficent female crowned him with laurel, while Fame lustily proclaimed the honours he had received, and unrolled the class-list in which his name had first rank.

Sweet land of visions, that will with such ease confer even a *treble* first upon the weary sleeper, why must he awake from thy gentle thraldom, to find the class-list a stern reality, and Graduateship too often but an empty dream!

4

Mr. Verdant Green Becomes
an Oxford Undergraduate

Mr. Verdant Green arose in the morning more or less refreshed; and after breakfast proceeded with his father to Brazenface College to call upon the Master; the porter directed them where to go, and they sent up their cards. Dr. Portman was at home, and they were soon introduced to his presence.

Instead of the stern, imposing-looking personage that Mr. Verdant Green had expected to see in the ruler among dons, and the terror of offending undergraduates, the master of Brazenface was a mild-looking old gentleman, with an inoffensive amiability of expression and a shy, retiring manner that seemed to intimate that he was more alarmed at the strangers than they had need to be at him. Dr. Portman seemed to be quite a part of his college, for he had passed the greatest portion of his life there. He had graduated there, he had taken Scholarships there, he had even gained a prize-poem there; he had been elected a Fellow there, he had become a

Tutor there, he had been Proctor and College Dean there; there, during the long vacation, he had written his celebrated 'Disquisition on the Greek Particles,' afterwards published in eight octavo volumes; and finally, there he had been elected Master of his college, in which office, honoured and respected, he appeared likely to end his days. He was unmarried; perhaps he had never found time to think of a wife; perhaps he had never had the courage to propose for one; perhaps he had met with early crosses and disappointments, and had shrined in his heart a fair image that should never be displaced. Who knows? for dons are mortals, and have been undergraduates once.

The little hair he had was of a silvery white, although his eye-brows retained their black hue; and to judge from the fine fresh-coloured features and the dark eyes that were now nervously twinkling upon Mr. Green, Dr. Portman must, in his more youthful days, have had an ample share of good looks. He was dressed in an old-fashioned reverend suit of black, with knee-breeches and gaiters, and a massive watch-seal dangling from under his waistcoat, and was deep in the study of his favourite particles. He received our hero and his father both nervously and graciously, and bade them be seated.

'I shall al-ways,' he said, in monosyllabic tones, as though he were reading out of a child's primer, — 'I shall al-ways be glad to see any of the young friends of my old col-lege friend Lar-kyns; and I do re-joice to be a-ble to serve you, Mis-ter Green; and I hope your son, Mis-ter, Mis-ter Vir — Vir-gin-ius, — '

'Verdant, Dr. Portman,' interrupted Mr. Green, suggestively, 'Verdant.'

'Oh! true, true, true! and I do hope that he will be a ve-ry good young man, and try to do hon-our to his col-lege.'

'I trust he will, indeed, sir,' replied Mr. Green; 'it is the great wish of my heart. And I am sure that you will find my son both quiet and orderly in his conduct, regular in his duties, and always in bed by ten o'clock.'

'Well, I hope so too, Mis-ter Green,' said Dr. Portman, monosyllabically; 'but all the young gen-tle-men do pro-mise to be regu-lar and or-der-ly when they first come up, but a term makes a great dif-fer-ence. But I dare say my young friend Mis-ter Vir-gin-ius, — '

'Verdant,' smilingly suggested Mr. Green.

'I beg your par-don,' apologized Dr. Portman; 'but I dare say that he will do as you say, for in-deed my friend Lar-kyns speaks well of him.'

'I am delighted — proud!' murmured Mr.

Green, while Verdant felt himself blushing up to his spectacles.

'We are ve-ry full,' Dr. Portman went on to say, 'but as I do ex-pect great things from Mis-ter Vir-gin — Verdant, Verdant, I have put some rooms at his ser-vice; and if you would like to see them, my ser-vant shall shew you the way.' The servant was accordingly summoned, and received orders to that effect; while the Master told Verdant that he must, at two o'clock, present himself to Mr. Slowcoach, his tutor, who would examine him for his matriculation.

'I am sor-ry, Mis-ter Green,' said Dr. Portman, 'that my en-gage-ments will pre-vent me from ask-ing you and Mis-ter Virg — Ver-dant, to dine with me to-day; but I do hope that the next time you come to Ox-ford I shall be more for-tu-nate.'

Old John, the Common-room man, who had heard this speech made to hundreds of 'governors' through many generations of freshmen, could not repress a few panto-mimic asides, that were suggestive of anything but full credence in his master's words. But Mr. Green was delighted with Dr. Portman's affability, and perceiving that the interview was at an end, made his *conge*, and left the Master of Brazenface to his Greek particles.

They had just got outside, when the

servant said, 'Oh, there is the scout! *Your* scout, sir!' at which our hero blushed from the consciousness of his new dignity; and, by way of appearing at his ease, inquired the scout's name.

'Robert Filcher, sir,' replied the servant; 'but the gentlemen always call 'em by their Christian names.' And beckoning the scout to him, he bade him shew the gentlemen to the rooms kept for Mr. Verdant Green; and then took himself back to the Master.

Mr. Robert Filcher might perhaps have been forty years of age, perhaps fifty; there was cunning enough in his face to fill even a century of wily years; and there was a depth of expression in his look, as he asked our hero if *he* was Mr. Verdant Green, that proclaimed his custom of reading a freshman at a glance. Mr. Filcher was laden with coats and boots that had just been brushed and blacked for their respective masters; and he was bearing a jug of Buttery ale (they are renowned for their ale at Brazenface) to the gentleman who owned the pair of 'tops' that were now flashing in the sun as they dangled from the scout's hand.

'Please to follow me, gentlemen,' he said; 'it's only just across the quad. Third floor, No. 4 staircase, fust quad; that's about the mark, *I* think, sir.'

Mr. Verdant Green glanced curiously round the Quadrangle, with its picturesque irregularity of outline, its towers and turrets and battlements, its grey time-eaten walls, its rows of mullioned heavy-headed windows, and the quiet cloistered air that spoke of study and reflection; and perceiving on one side a row of large windows, with great buttresses between, and a species of steeple on the high-pitched roof, he made bold (just to try the effect) to address Mr. Filcher by the name assigned to him at an early period of his life by his godfathers and godmothers, and inquired if that building was the chapel.

'No, sir,' replied Robert, 'that there's the 'All, sir, *that* is — where you dines, sir, leastways when you ain't 'AEger,' or elseweer. That at the top is the lantern, sir, *that* is; called so because it never has no candle in it. The chapel's the hopposite side, sir. - Please not to walk on the grass, sir; there's a fine agen it, unless you're a Master. This way if *you* please, gentlemen!' Thus the scout beguiled them, as he led them to an open doorway with a large 4 painted over it; inside was a door on either hand, while a coal-bin displayed its black face from under a staircase that rose immediately before them. Up this they went, following the scout (who had vanished for a moment with the boots and beer), and when they had passed the first floor they found the ascent by no means easy to the body, or pleasant to the sight. The once white-washed walls were coated with the uncleansed dust of the three past terms; and where the plaster had not been chipped off by flying porter-bottles, or the heels of Wellington boots, its surface had afforded an irresistible temptation to those imaginative undergraduates who displayed their artistic genius in candle-smoke cartoons of the heads of the University, and other popular and unpopular characters. All Mr. Green's caution, as he crept up the dark, twisting staircase, could not prevent him from crushing his hat against the low, cobwebbed ceiling, and he gave vent to a very strong but quiet anathema, which glided quietly and audibly into the remark, 'Confounded awkward staircase, I think!'

'Just what Mr. Bouncer says,' replied the scout, 'although he don't reach so high as you, sir; but he *do* say, sir, when he comes home pleasant at night from some wine-party, that it *is* the aukardest staircase as was ever put before a gentleman's legs. And he *did* go so far, sir, as to ask the Master, if it wouldn't be better to have a staircase as would go up of hisself, and take the gentlemen up with it, like one as they has at some public show in London — the Call-and-see-em, I think he said.'

'The Colosseum, probably,' suggested Mr. Green. 'And what did Dr. Portman say to that, pray?'

'Why he said, sir, — leastways so Mr. Bouncer reported, — that it worn't by no means a bad idea, and that p'raps Mr. Bouncer'd find it done in six months' time, when he come back again from the country. For you see, sir, Mr. Bouncer had made hisself so pleasant, that he'd been and got the porter out o' bed, and corked his face dreadful; and then, sir, he'd been and got a Hinn-board from somewhere out of the town, and hung it on the Master's private door; so that when they went to early chapel in the morning, they read as how the Master was 'licensed to sell beer by retail,' and 'to be drunk on the premises'. So when the Master came to know who it was as did it, which in course the porter told him, he said as how Mr. Bouncer had better go down into the country for a year, for change of air, and to visit his friends.'

'Very kind indeed of Dr. Portman,' said our hero, who missed the moral of the story, and took the rustication for a kind forgiveness of injuries.

'Just what Mr. Bouncer said, sir,' replied

the scout, 'he said it were pertickler kind and thoughtful. This is his room, sir, he come up on'y yesterday.' And he pointed to a door, above which was painted in white letters on a black ground, 'BOUNCER.'

'Why,' said Mr. Green to his son, 'now I think of it, Bouncer was the name of that short young gentleman who came with us on the coach yesterday, and made himself so — so unpleasant with a tin horn.'

'That's the gent, sir,' observed the scout; 'that's Mr. Bouncer, agoing the complete unicorn, as he calls it. I dare say you'll find him a pleasant neighbour, sir. Your rooms is next to his.'

With some doubts of these prospective pleasures, the Mr. Greens, *pere et fils*, entered through a double door painted over the outside, with the name of 'SMALLS'; to which Mr. Filcher directed our hero's attention by saying, 'You can have that name took out, sir, and your own name painted in. Mr. Smalls has just moved hisself to the other quad, and that's why the rooms is vacant, sir.'

Mr. Filcher then went on to point out the properties and capabilities of the rooms, and also their mechanical contrivances.

'This is the hoak, this 'ere outer door is, sir, which the gentlemen sports, that is to say, shuts, sir, when they're a readin'. Not as Mr.

Smalls ever hinterfered with his constitootion by too much 'ard study, sir; he only sported his hoak when people used to get troublesome about their little bills. Here's a place for coals, sir, though Mr. Smalls, he kept his bull-terrier there, which was agin the regulations, as *you* know, sir.' (Verdant nodded his head, as though he were perfectly aware of the fact.) 'This ere's your bed-room, sir. Very small, did you say, sir? Oh, no, sir; not by no means! We thinks that in college reether a biggish bed-room, sir. Mr. Smalls thought so, sir, and he's in his second year, *he* is.' (Mr. Filcher thoroughly understood the science of 'flooring' a freshman.)

'This is *my* room, sir, this is, for keepin' your cups and saucers, and wine-glasses and tumblers, and them sort o' things, and washin' 'em up when you wants 'em. If you likes to keep your wine and sperrits here, sir — Mr. Smalls always did — you'll find it a nice cool place, sir: or else here's this 'ere winder-seat; you see, sir, it opens with a lid, 'andy for the purpose.'

'If you act upon that suggestion, Verdant,' remarked Mr. Green aside to his son, 'I trust that a lock will be added.'

There was not a superfluity of furniture in the room; and Mr. Smalls having conveyed away the luxurious part of it, that which was left had more of the useful than the ornamental character; but as Mr. Verdant Green was no Sybarite, this point was but of little consequence.

The window looked with a sunny aspect down upon the quad, and over the opposite buildings were seen the spires of churches, the dome of the Radcliffe, and the gables, pinnacles, and turrets of other colleges. This was pleasant enough: pleasanter than the stale odours of the Virginian weed that rose from the faded green window-curtains, and from the old Kidderminster carpet that had been charred and burnt into holes with the fag-ends of cigars.

'Well, Verdant,' said Mr. Green, when they had completed their inspection, 'the rooms are not so very bad, and I think you may be able to make yourself comfortable in them. But I wish they were not so high up. I don't see how you can escape if a fire was to break out, and I am afraid collegians must be very careless on these points. Indeed, your mother made me promise that I would speak to Dr. Portman about it, and ask him to please allow your tutor, or somebody, to see that your fire was safely raked out at night; and I had intended to have done so, but somehow it quite escaped me. How your mother and all at home would like to see you in your own college room!' And the thoughts of father and son flew back to the Manor Green and its occupants, who were doubtless at the same time thinking of them.

Mr. Filcher then explained the system of thirds, by which the furniture of the room was to be paid for; and, having accompanied his future master and Mr. Green downstairs, the latter accomplishing the descent not without difficulty and contusions, and having pointed out the way to Mr. Slowcoach's rooms, Mr. Robert Filcher relieved his feelings by indulging in a ballet of action, or *pas d'extase*; in which poetry of motion he declared his joy at the last valuable addition to Brazenface, and his own perquisites.

Mr. Slowcoach was within, and would see Mr. Verdant Green. So that young gentleman, trembling with agitation, and feeling as though he would have given pounds for the staircase to have been as high as that of Babel, followed the servant upstairs, and left his father, in almost as great a state of nervousness, pacing the quad below. But it was not the formidable affair, nor was Mr. Slowcoach the formidable man, that Mr. Verdant Green had anticipated; and by the time that he had turned a piece of *Spectator* into Latin, our hero had somewhat recovered his usual equanimity of mind and serenity of expression: and the construing of half a dozen lines of Livy and Homer, and the answering of a few questions, was a mere form; for Mr. Slowcoach's long practice enabled him to see in a very few minutes if the freshman before him (however nervous he might be) had the usual average of abilities, and was up to the business of lectures. So Mr. Verdant Green was soon dismissed, and returned to his father radiant and happy.

5

Mr. Verdant Green Matriculates, and Makes a Sensation

As they went out at the gate, they inquired of the porter for Mr. Charles Larkyns, but they found that he had not yet returned from the friend's house where he had been during the vacation; whereupon Mr. Green said that they would go and look at the Oxford lions, so that he might be able to answer any of the questions that should be put to him on his return.

They soon found a guide, one of those wonderful people to which show-places give birth, and of whom Oxford can boast a very goodly average; and under this gentleman's guidance Mr. Verdant Green made his first acquaintance with the fair outside of his Alma Mater.

The short, thick stick of the guide served to direct attention to the various objects he enumerated in his rapid career: 'This here's Christ Church College,' he said, as he trotted them down St Aldate's, 'built by Card'nal Hoolsy four underd feet long and the famous

Tom Tower as tolls wun underd and wun hevery night that being the number of stoodents on the foundation;' and thus the guide went on, perfectly independent of the artificial trammels of punctuation, and not particular whether his hearers understood him or not: that was not *his* business. And as it was that gentleman's boast that he 'could do the alls, collidges, and principal hedifices in a nour and a naff,' it could not be expected but that Mr. Green should take back to Warwickshire otherwise than a slightly confused impression of Oxford.

When he unrolled that rich panorama before his 'mind's eye,' all its component parts were strangely out of place. The rich spire of St. Mary's claimed acquaintance with her poorer sister at the cathedral.

The cupola of the Tom Tower got into close quarters with the huge dome of the Radcliffe, that shrugged up its great round shoulders at the intrusion of the cross-bred Graeco-Gothic tower of All Saints. The theatre had walked up to St. Giles's to see how the Taylor Buildings agreed with the University galleries; while the Martyrs' Memorial had stepped down to Magdalen Bridge, in time to see the college taking a walk in the Botanic Gardens. The Schools and the Bodleian had set their back against the stately portico of the

Clarendon Press; while the antiquated Ashmolean had given place to the more modern Townhall. The time-honoured, black-looking front of University College had changed into the cold cleanliness of the 'classic' *facade* of Queen's. The two towers of All Souls' — whose several stages seem to be pulled out of each other like the parts of a telescope, — had, somehow, removed themselves from the rest of the building, which had gone, nevertheless, on a tour to Broad Street; behind which, as every one knows, are the Broad Walk and the Christ Church meadows. Merton Chapel had got into *New* quarters; and Wadham had gone to Worcester for change of air. Lincoln had migrated from near Exeter to Pembroke; and Brasenose had its nose quite put out of joint by St. John's. In short, if the maps of Oxford are to be trusted, there had been a general *pousset* movement among its public buildings.

But if such a shrewd and practised observer as Sir Walter Scott, after a week's hard and systematic sight-seeing, could only say of Oxford, 'The time has been much too short to convey to me separate and distinct ideas of all the variety of wonders that I saw: my memory only at present furnishes a grand but indistinct picture of towers, and chapels, and oriels, and vaulted halls, and libraries, and paintings;' — if Sir Walter Scott could say this after a week's work, it is not to be wondered at that Mr. Green, after so brief and rapid a survey of the city at the heels of an unintelligent guide, should feel himself slightly confused when, on his return to the Manor Green, he attempted to give a slight description of the wonderful sights of Oxford.

There was one lion of Oxford, however, whose individuality of expression was too striking either to be forgotten or confused with the many other lions around. Although (as in Byron's *Dream*)

'A mass of many images
Crowded like waves upon'

Mr. Green, yet clear and distinct through all there ran

'The stream-like windings of that glorious street,'

to which one of the first critics of the age has given this high testimony of praise: 'The High Street of Oxford has not its equal in the whole world.'

Mr. Green could not, of course, leave Oxford until he had seen his beloved son in that elegant cap and preposterous gown which constitute the present academical dress of the Oxford undergraduate; and to assume which, with a legal right to the same, matriculation is first necessary. As that amusing and instructive book, the *University Statutes*, says in its own delightful and unrivalled canine Latin, '*Statutum est, quod nemo pro Studente, seu Scholari, habeatur, nec ullis Universitatis privilegiis, aut beneficiis*' (the cap and gown, of course, being among these), '*gaudeat, nisi qui in aliquod Collegium vel Aulam admissus fuerit, et intra quindenam post talem admissionem in matriculam Universitatis fuerit relatus.*' So our hero put on the required white tie, and then went forth to complete his proper costume.

There were so many persons purporting to be 'Academical robe-makers,' that Mr. Green was some little time in deciding who should be the tradesman favoured with the order for his son's adornment. At last he fixed upon a shop, the window of which contained a more imposing display than its neighbours of gowns, hoods, surplices, and robes of all shapes and colours, from the black velvet-sleeved proctor's to the blushing gorgeousness of the scarlet robe and crimson silk sleeves of the D.C.L.

'I wish you,' said Mr. Green, advancing towards a smirking individual, who was in his shirt-sleeves and slippers, but in all other respects was attired with great magnificence, — 'I wish you to measure this gentleman for his academical robes, and also to allow him the use of some to be matriculated in.'

'Certainly, sir,' said the robe-maker, who stood bowing and smirking before them — as Hood expressively says,

'Washing his hands with invisible soap,
In imperceptible water;' —

'certainly, sir, if you wish it: but it will scarcely be necessary, sir; as our custom is so extensive, that we keep a large ready-made stock constantly on hand.'

'Oh, that will do just as well,' said Mr. Green; 'better, indeed. Let us see some.'

'What description of robe would be required?' said the smirking gentleman, again making use of the invisible soap; 'a scholar's?'

'A scholar's!' repeated Mr. Green, very much wondering at the question, and imagining that all students must of necessity be also scholars; 'yes, a scholar's, of course.'

A scholar's gown was accordingly produced: and its deep, wide sleeves, and ample length and breadth, were soon displayed to some advantage on Mr. Verdant Green's tall figure. Reflected in a large mirror, its charms were seen in their full perfection; and when the delighted Mr. Green exclaimed, 'Why, Verdant, I never saw you look so well as you do now!' our hero was inclined to think that his father's words were the words of truth, and that a scholar's gown was indeed becoming. The *tout ensemble* was complete when the cap had been added to the gown; more especially as Verdant put it on in such a manner that the polite robe-maker was obliged to say, 'The hother way, if you please, sir. Immaterial perhaps, but generally preferred. In fact, the shallow part is *always* the forehead, — at least, in Oxford, sir.'

While Mr. Green was paying for the cap and gown (N.B. the money of governors is never refused), the robe-maker smirked, and said, 'Hexcuse the question; but may I hask, sir, if this is the gentleman that has just gained the Scotland Scholarship?'

'No,' replied Mr. Green. 'My son has just gained his matriculation, and, I believe, very creditably; but nothing more, as we only came here yesterday.'

'Then I think, sir,' said the robe-maker, with redoubled smirks — 'I think, sir, there is a leetle mistake here. The gentleman will be hinfringing the University statues, if he wears a scholar's gown and hasn't got a scholarship; and these robes'll be of no use to the gentleman, yet awhile at least. It will be an undergraduate's gown that he requires, sir.'

It was fortunate for our hero that the mistake was discovered so soon, and could be rectified without any of those unpleasant consequences of iconoclasm to which the robe-maker's infringement of the 'statues' seemed to point; but as that gentleman put the scholar's gown on one side, and brought out a commoner's, he might have been heard to mutter, 'I don't know which is the freshest, — the freshman or his guv'nor.'

When Mr. Verdant Green once more looked in the glass, and saw hanging straight from his shoulders a yard of blueish-black stuff, garnished with a little lappet, and two streamers whose upper parts were gathered into double plaits, he regretted that he was not indeed a scholar, if it were only for the privilege of wearing so elegant a gown. However, his father smiled approvingly, the robe-maker smirked judiciously; so he came to the gratifying conclusion that the commoner's gown was by no means ugly, and would be thought a great deal of at the Manor Green when he took it home at the end of the term.

Leaving his hat with the robe-maker, who, with many more smirks and imaginary washings of the hands, hoped to be favoured with the gentleman's patronage on future occasions, and begged further to trouble him with a card of his establishment, — our hero proceeded with his father along the High Street, and turned round by St. Mary's, and so up Cat Street to the Schools, where they made their way to the classic 'Pig-market,' to await the arrival of the Vice-Chancellor.

When he came, our freshman and two other white-tied fellow-freshmen were summoned to the great man's presence; and there, in the ante-chamber of the Convocation House, the edifying and imposing spectacle of Matriculation was enacted. In the first place, Mr. Verdant Green took divers oaths, and sincerely promised and swore that he would be faithful and bear true allegiance to her Majesty Queen Victoria. He also professed (very much to his own astonishment) that he did 'from his heart abhor, detest, and abjure, as impious and heretical, that damnable doctrine and position, that princes excommunicated or deprived by the pope, or any authority of the see of Rome, may be deposed or murdered by their subjects, or any other whatsoever.' And, having almost lost his breath at this novel 'position,' Mr. Verdant Green could only gasp his declaration, 'that no foreign prince, person, prelate, state, or potentate, hath, or ought to have, any jurisdiction, power, superiority, pre-eminence, or authority, ecclesiastical or spiritual, within this realm.' When he had sufficiently recovered his presence of mind, Mr. Verdant Green inserted his name in the University books as 'Generosi filius natu maximus'; and then signed his name to the Thirty-nine Articles, — though he did not endanger his matriculation, as Theodore Hook did, by professing his readiness to sign forty if they wished it! Then the Vice-Chancellor concluded the performance by presenting to the three freshmen (in the most liberal manner) three brown-looking volumes, with these words: 'Scitote vos in Matriculam Universitatis hodie relatos esse, sub hac conditione, nempe ut omnia Statuta hoc libro comprehensa pro virili observetis.' And the ceremony was at an end, and Mr. Verdant Green was a matriculated member of the University of Oxford. He was far too nervous, — from the weakening effect of the popes, and the excommunicate princes, and their murderous subjects, — to be able to translate and understand what the Vice-Chancellor had said to him, but he thought his present to be particularly kind; and he found it a copy of the University Statutes, which he determined forthwith to read and obey.

Though if he had known that he had sworn

to observe statutes which required him, among other things, to wear garments only of a black or 'subfusk' hue; to abstain from that absurd and proud custom of walking in public *in boots*, and the ridiculous one of wearing the hair long; — statutes, moreover, which demanded of him to refrain from all taverns, wine-shops, and houses in which they sold wine or any other drink, and the herb called nicotiana or 'tobacco'; not to hunt wild beasts with dogs or snares or nets; not to carry cross-bows or other 'bombarding' weapons, or keep hawks for fowling; not to frequent theatres or the strifes of gladiators; and only to carry a bow and arrows for the sake of honest recreation; — if Mr. Verdant Green had known that he had covenanted to do this, he would, perhaps, have felt some scruples in taking the oaths of matriculation. But this by the way.

Now that Mr. Green had seen all that he wished to see, nothing remained for him but to discharge his hotel bill. It was accordingly called for, and produced by the waiter, whose face — by a visitation of that complaint against which vaccination is usually considered a safeguard — had been reduced to a state resembling the interior half of a sliced muffin. To judge from the expression of Mr. Green's features as he regarded the document

71

that had been put into his hand, it is probable that he had not been much accustomed to Oxford hotels; for he ran over the several items of the bill with a look in which surprise contended with indignation for the mastery, while the muffin-faced waiter handled his plated salver, and looked fixedly at nothing.

Mr. Green, however, refraining from observations, paid the bill; and, muffling himself in greatcoat and travelling-cap, he prepared himself to take a comfortable journey back to Warwickshire, inside the Birmingham and Oxford coach. It was not loaded in the same way that it had been when he came up by it, and his fellow-passengers were of a very different description; and it must be confessed that, in the absence of Mr. Bouncer's tin horn, the attacks of intrusive terriers, and the involuntary fumigation of himself with tobacco (although its presence was still perceptible within the coach), Mr. Green found his journey *from* Oxford much more agreeable than it had been *to* that place. He took an affectionate farewell of his son, somewhat after the manner of the 'heavy fathers' of the stage; and then the coach bore him away from the last lingering look of our hero, who felt any thing but heroic at being left for the first time in his life to shift for himself.

His luggage had been sent up to Brazen-face, so thither he turned his steps, and with some little difficulty found his room. Mr. Filcher had partly unpacked his master's things, and had left everything uncomfortable and in 'the most admired disorder'; and Mr. Verdant Green sat himself down upon the 'practicable' window-seat, and resigned himself to his thoughts. If they had not already flown to the Manor Green, they would soon have been carried there; for a German band, just outside the college-gates, began to play 'Home, sweet home,' with that truth and delicacy of expression which the wandering minstrels of Germany seem to acquire intuitively. The sweet melancholy of the simple air, as it came subdued by distance into softer tones, would have powerfully affected most people who had just been torn from the bosom of their homes, to fight, all inexperienced, the battle of life; but it had such an effect on Mr. Verdant Green, that — but it little matters saying *what* he did; many people will give way to feelings in private that they would stifle in company; and if Mr. Filcher on his return found his master wiping his spectacles, why that was only a simple proceeding which all glasses frequently require.

To divert his thoughts, and to impress

upon himself and others the fact that he was an Oxford MAN, our freshman set out for a stroll; and as the unaccustomed feeling of the gown about his shoulders made him feel somewhat embarrassed as to the carriage of his arms, he stepped into a shop on the way and purchased a light cane, which he considered would greatly add to the effect of the cap and gown.

Armed with this weapon, he proceeded to disport himself in the Christ Church meadows, and promenaded up and down the Broad Walk.

The beautiful meadows lay green and bright in the sun; the arching trees threw a softened light, and made a chequered pavement of the great Broad Walk; 'witch-elms *did* counter-change the floor' of the gravel-walks that wound with the windings of the Cherwell; the drooping willows were mirrored in its stream; through openings in the trees there were glimpses of grey, old college-buildings; then came the walk along the banks, the Isis shining like molten silver, and fringed around with barges and boats; then another stretch of green meadows; then a cloud of steam from the railway-station; and a background of gently-rising hills. It was a cheerful scene, and the variety of figures gave life and animation to the whole.

Young ladies and unprotected females were found in abundance, dressed in all the engaging variety of light spring dresses; and, as may be supposed, our hero attracted a great deal of their attention, and afforded them no small amusement. But the unusual and terrific appearance of a spectacled gownsman with a cane produced the greatest alarm among the juveniles, who imagined our freshman to be a new description of beadle or Bogy, summoned up by the exigencies of the times to preserve a rigorous discipline among the young people; and, regarding his cane as the symbol of his stern sway, they harassed their nursemaids by unceasingly charging at their petticoats for protection.

Altogether, Mr. Verdant Green made quite a sensation.

6

Mr. Verdant Green Dines,
Breakfasts and Goes to Chapel

Our hero dressed himself with great care, that
he might make his first appearance in Hall
with proper *eclat* — and, having made his
way towards the lantern-surmounted building, he walked up the steps and under the
groined archway with a crowd of hungry
undergraduates who were hurrying in to
dinner. The clatter of plates would have alone
been sufficient to guide his steps; and, passing
through one of the doors in the elaborately
carved screen that shut off the passage and
the buttery, he found himself within the hall
of Brazenface. It was of noble size, lighted by
lofty windows, and carried up to a great
height by an open roof, dark (save where it
opened to the lantern) with great oak beams,
and rich with carved pendants and gilded
bosses. The ample fire-places displayed the
capaciousness of those collegiate mouths of
'the wind-pipes of hospitality,' and gave an
idea of the dimensions of the kitchen ranges.
In the centre of the hall was a huge

plate-warmer, elaborately worked in brass with the college arms. Founders and benefactors were seen, or suggested, on all sides; their arms gleamed from the windows in all the glories of stained glass; and their faces peered out from the massive gilt frames on the walls, as though their shadows loved to linger about the spot that had been benefited by their substance. At the further end of the hall a deep bay-window threw its painted light upon a dais, along which stretched the table for the Dons; Masters and Bachelors occupied side-tables; and the other tables were filled up by the undergraduates; every one, from the Don downwards, being in his gown.

Our hero was considerably impressed with the (to him) singular character of the scene; and from the 'Benedictus benedicat' grace-before-meat to the 'Benedicto benedicamur' after-meat, he gazed curiously around him in silent wonderment. So much indeed was he wrapped up in the novelty of the scene, that he ran a great risk of losing his dinner. The scouts fled about in all directions with plates, and glasses, and pewter dishes, and massive silver mugs that had gone round the tables for the last two centuries, and still no one waited upon Mr. Verdant Green. He twice ventured to timidly say, 'Waiter!' but as no one answered to his call, and as he was too bashful and occupied with his own thoughts to make another attempt, it is probable that he would have risen from dinner as unsatisfied as when he sat down, had not his right-hand companion (having partly relieved his own wants) perceived his neighbour to be a freshman, and kindly said to him, 'I think you'd better begin your dinner, because we don't stay here long. What is your scout's name?' And when he had been told it, he turned to Mr. Filcher and asked him, 'What the doose he meant by not waiting on his master?' which, with the addition of a few gratuitous threats, had the effect of bringing that gentleman to his master's side, and reducing Mr. Verdant Green to a state of mind in which gratitude to his companion and a desire to beg his scout's pardon were confusedly blended. Not seeing any dishes upon the table to select from, he referred to the list, and fell back on the standard roast beef.

'I am sure I am very much obliged to you,' said Verdant, turning to his friendly neighbour. 'My rooms are next to yours, and I had the pleasure of being driven by you on the coach the other day.'

'Oh!' said Mr. Fosbrooke, for it was he; 'ah, I remember you now! I suppose the old bird was your governor. *He* seemed to think it any thing but a pleasure, being driven by Four-in-hand Fosbrooke.'

'Why, pap — my father — is rather nervous on a coach,' replied Verdant: 'he was bringing me to college for the first time.'

'Then you are the man that has just come into Smalls' old rooms? Oh, I see. Don't you ever drink with your dinner? If you don't holler for your rascal, he'll never half wait upon you. Always bully them well at first, and then they learn manners.'

So, by way of commencing the bullying system without loss of time, our hero called out very fiercely 'Robert!' and then, as Mr. Filcher glided to his side, he timidly dropped his tone into a mild 'Glass of water, if you please, Robert.'

He felt rather relieved when dinner was over, and retired at once to his own rooms; where, making a rather quiet and sudden entrance, he found them tenanted by an old woman, who wore a huge bonnet tilted on the top of her head, and was busily and dubiously engaged at one of his open boxes. 'Ahem!' he coughed, at which note of warning the old lady jumped round very quickly, and said, — dabbing curtseys where there were stops, like the beats of a conductor's *baton*, — 'Law bless me, sir. It's beggin' your parding that I am. Not seein' you a comin' in. Bein' 'ard of hearin' from a hinfant. And havin' my back turned. I was just a puttin' your things to rights, sir. If you please, sir, I'm Mrs. Tester. Your bed-maker, sir.'

'Oh, thank you,' said our freshman, with the shadow of a suspicion that Mrs. Tester was doing something more than merely 'putting to rights' the pots of jam and marmalade, and the packages of tea and coffee, which his doting mother had thoughtfully placed in his box as a provision against immediate distress. 'Thank you.'

'I've done my rooms, sir,' dabbed Mrs. Tester. 'Which if thought agreeable, I'd stay and put these things in their places. Which it certainly is Robert's place. But I never minds putting myself out. As I always perpetually am minded. So long as I can obleege the gentlemen.'

So, as our hero was of a yielding disposition, and could, under skilful hands, easily be moulded into any form, he allowed Mrs. Tester to remain, and conclude the unpacking and putting away of his goods, in which operations she displayed great generalship.

'You've a deal of tea and coffee, sir,' she said, keeping time by curtseys. 'Which it's a great blessin' to have a mother. And not to be left dissolute like some gentlemen. And tea and coffee is what I mostly lives on. And mortial dear it is to poor folks. And a package the likes of this, sir, were a blessin' should never even dream on.'

'Well, then,' said Verdant, in a most benevolent mood, 'you can take one of the packages for your trouble.'

Upon this, Mrs. Tester appeared to be greatly overcome. 'Which I once had a son myself,' she said. 'And as fine a young man as you are, sir. With a strawberry mark in the small of his back. And beautiful red whiskers, sir; with a tendency to drink. Which it were his rewing, and took him to be enlisted for a sojer. When he went across the seas to the West Injies. And was took with the yaller fever, and buried there. Which the remembrance, sir, brings on my spazzums. To which I'm an hafflicted martyr, sir. And can only be heased with three spots of brandy on a lump of sugar. Which your good mother, sir, has put a bottle of brandy. Along with the jam and the clean linen, sir. As though a purpose for my complaint. Ugh! oh!'

And Mrs. Tester forthwith began pressing and thumping her sides in such a terrific manner, and appeared to be undergoing such internal agony, that Mr. Verdant Green not only gave her brandy there and then, for her immediate relief — 'which it heases the spazzums deerectly, bless you,' observed Mrs. Tester, parenthetically; but also told her where she could find the bottle, in case she should again be attacked when in his rooms; attacks which, it is needless to say, were repeated at every subsequent visit. Mrs. Tester then finished putting away the tea and coffee, and entered into further particulars about her late son; though what connection there was between him and the packages of tea, our hero could not perceive. Nevertheless he was much interested with her narrative, and thought Mrs. Tester a very affectionate, motherly sort of woman; more especially, when (Robert having placed his tea-things on the table) she showed him how to make the tea; an apparently simple feat that the freshman found himself perfectly unable to accomplish. And then Mrs. Tester made a final dab, and her exit, and our hero sat over his tea as long as he could, because it gave an idea of cheerfulness; and then, after directing Robert to be sure not to forget to call him in time for morning chapel, he retired to bed.

The bed was very hard, and so small, that, had it not been for the wall, our hero's legs would have been visible (literally) at the foot; but despite these novelties, he sank into a sound rest, which at length passed into the following dream. He thought that he was back again at dinner at the Manor Green, but that the room was curiously like the hall of Brazenface, and that Mrs. Tester and Dr. Portman were on either side of him, with Mr. Fosbrooke and Robert talking to his sisters; and that he was reaching his hand to help Mrs. Tester to a packet of tea, which her son had sent them from the West Indies, when he threw over a wax-light, and set every thing on fire; and that the parish engine came up; and that there was a great noise, and a loud hammering; and, 'Eh? yes! oh! the half-hour is it? Oh, yes! thank you!' And Mr. Verdant Green sprang out of bed much relieved in mind to find that the alarm of fire was nothing more than his scout knocking vigorously at his door, and that it was chapel-time.

'Want any warm water, sir?' asked Mr. Filcher, putting his head in at the door.

'No, thank you,' replied our hero; 'I — I — '

'Shave with cold. Ah! I see, sir. It's much 'ealthier, and makes the 'air grow. But any thing as you *does* want, sir, you've only to call.'

'If there is any thing that I want, Robert,' said Verdant, 'I will ring.'

'Bless you, sir,' observed Mr. Filcher, 'there ain't no bells never in colleges! They'd be rung off their wires in no time. Mr. Bouncer, sir, he uses a trumpet like they does on board ship. By the same token, that's it, sir!' And Mr. Filcher vanished, just in time to prevent little Mr. Bouncer from finishing a furious solo, from an entirely new version of *Robert le Diable*, which he was giving with novel effects through the medium of a speaking-trumpet.

Verdant found his bed-room inconveniently small; so contracted, indeed, in its dimensions, that his toilette was not completed without his elbows having first suffered severe abrasions. His mechanical turnip shewed him that he had no time to lose, and the furious ringing of a bell, whose noise was echoed by the bells of other colleges, made him dress with a rapidity quite unusual, and hurry down stairs and across quad, to the chapel steps, up which a throng of students were hastening. Nearly all betrayed symptoms of having been aroused from their sleep without having had any spare time for an elaborate toilette, and many, indeed, were completing it, by thrusting themselves into surplices and gowns as they hurried up the steps.

Mr. Fosbrooke was one of these; and when he saw Verdant close to him, he benevolently recognized him, and said, 'Let me put you up to a wrinkle. When they ring you up sharp for chapel, don't you lose any time about your absolutions, — washing, you know; but just jump into a pair of bags and Wellingtons; clap a top-coat on you, and button it up to the chin, and there you are, ready dressed in the twinkling of a bed-post.'

Before Mr. Verdant Green could at all comprehend why a person should jump into two bags, instead of dressing himself in the normal manner, they went through the ante-chapel, or 'Court of the Gentiles,' as Mr. Fosbrooke termed it, and entered the choir of the chapel through a screen elaborately decorated in the Jacobean style, with pillars and arches, and festoons of fruit and flowers, and bells and pomegranates. On either side of the door were two men, who quickly glanced at each one who passed, and as quickly pricked a mark against his name on the chapel lists. As the freshman went by, they made a careful study of his person, and took mental daguerreotypes of his features. Seeing no beadle, or pew-opener (or, for the matter of that, any pews), or any one to direct him to a place, Mr. Verdant Green quietly took a seat in the first place that he found empty, which happened to be the stall on the right hand of the door.

Unconscious of the trespass he was committing, he at once put his cap to his face and knelt down; but he had no sooner risen from his knees, than he found an imposing-looking Don, as large as life and quite as natural, who was staring at him with the greatest astonishment, and motioning him to immediately 'come out of that!' This our hero did with the greatest speed and confusion, and sank breathless on the end of the nearest bench; when, just as in his agitation, he had again said his prayer, the service fortunately commenced, and somewhat relieved him of his embarrassment.

Although he had the glories of Magdalen, Merton, and New College chapels fresh in his mind, yet Verdant was considerably impressed with the solemn beauties of his own college chapel. He admired its harmonious proportions, and the elaborate carving of its decorated tracery. He noted every thing: the great eagle that seemed to be spreading its wings for an upward flight, — the pavement of black and white marble, — the dark canopied stalls, rich with the later work of Grinling Gibbons, — the elegant tracery of the windows; and he lost himself in a solemn reverie as he looked up at the saintly forms through which the rays of the morning sun streamed in rainbow tints.

But the lesson had just begun; and the man on Verdant's right appeared to be attentively following it. Our freshman, however, could not help seeing the book, and, much to his astonishment, he found it to be a Livy, out of which his neighbour was getting up his morning's lecture. He was still more astonished, when the lesson had come to an end, by being suddenly pulled back when he attempted to rise, and finding the streamers of his gown had been put to a use never intended for them, by being tied round the finial of the stall behind him, — the silly work of a boyish gentleman, who, in his desire to play off a practical joke on a freshman, forgot the sacredness of the place where college rules compelled him to shew himself on morning parade.

Chapel over, our hero hurried back to his rooms, and there, to his great joy, found a budget of letters from home; and surely the little items of intelligence that made up the news of the Manor Green had never seemed to possess such interest as now! The reading and re-reading of these occupied him during the whole of breakfast-time; and Mr. Filcher found him still engaged in perusing them when he came to clear away the things.

Then it was that Verdant discovered the extended meaning that the word 'perquisites' possesses in the eyes of a scout, for, to a remark that he had made, Robert replied in a tone of surprise, 'Put away these bits o' things as is left, sir!' and then added, with an air of mild correction, 'you see, sir, you's fresh to the place, and don't know that gentlemen never likes that sort o' thing done *here*, sir; but you gets your commons, sir, fresh and fresh every morning and evening, which must be much more agreeable to the 'ealth than a heating of stale bread and such like. No, sir!' continued Mr. Filcher, with a manner that was truly parental, 'no sir! you trust to me, sir, and I'll take care of your things, I will.' And from the way that he carried off the eatables, it seemed probable that he would make good his words. But our freshman felt considerable awe of his scout, and murmuring broken accents, that sounded like 'ignorance — customs — University,' he endeavoured, by a liberal use of his pocket-handkerchief, to appear as if he were not blushing.

As Mr. Slowcoach had told him that he would not have to begin lectures until the following day, and as the Greek play fixed for the lecture was one with which he had been made well acquainted by Mr. Larkyns,

Verdant began to consider what he could do with himself, when the thought of Mr. Larkyns suggested the idea that his son Charles had probably by this time returned to college. He determined therefore at once to go in search of him; and looking out a letter which the rector had commissioned him to deliver to his son, he inquired of Robert, if he was aware whether Mr. Charles Larkyns had come back from his holidays.

'"Ollidays, sir?,' said Mr. Filcher. 'Oh! I see, sir! Vacation, you mean, sir. Young gentlemen as is *men*, sir, likes to call their 'ollidays by a different name to boys', sir. Yes, sir, Mr. Charles Larkyns, he come up last arternoon, sir; but he and Mr. Smalls, the gent as he's been down with this vacation, the same as had these rooms, sir, they didn't come to 'All, sir, but went and had their dinners comfortable at the Star, sir; and very pleasant they made theirselves; and Thomas, their scout, sir, has had quite a horder for sober-water this morning, sir.'

With somewhat of a feeling of wonder how one scout contrived to know so much of the proceedings of gentlemen who were waited on by another scout, and wholly ignorant of his allusion to his fellow-servant's dealings in soda-water, Mr. Verdant Green inquired where he could find Mr. Larkyns, and as the

89

rooms were but just on the other side of the quad., he put on his hat, and made his way to them. The scout was just going into the room, so our hero gave a tap at the door and followed him.

7

Mr. Verdant Green Calls on a Gentleman Who Is Licensed to Sell

Mr. Verdant Green found himself in a room that had a pleasant look-out over the gardens of Brazenface, from which a noble chestnut tree brought its pyramids of bloom close up to the very windows. The walls of the room were decorated with engravings in gilt frames, their variety of subject denoting the catholic taste of their proprietor. 'The start for the Derby,' and other coloured hunting prints, shewed his taste for the field and horseflesh; Landseer's 'Distinguished Member of the Humane Society,' 'Dignity and Impudence,' and others, displayed his fondness for dog-flesh; while Byron beauties, 'Amy Robsart,' and some extremely *au naturel* pets of the ballet, proclaimed his passion for the fair sex in general. Over the fire-place was a mirror (for Mr. Charles Larkyns was not averse to the reflection of his good-looking features, and was rather glad than otherwise of 'an excuse for the glass,') its frame stuck full of tradesmen's cards and (unpaid) bills, invites, 'bits of pasteboard' pencilled with a mystic 'wine,' and other odds and ends: — no private letters though! Mr. Larkyns was too wary to leave his 'family secrets' for the delectation of his scout. Over the mirror was displayed a fox's mask, gazing vacantly from between two brushes; leaving the spectator to imagine that Mr. Charles Larkyns was a second Nimrod, and had in some way or other been intimately concerned in the capture of these trophies of the chase. This supposition of the imaginative spectator would be strengthened by the appearance of a list of hunting appointments (of the past season) pinned up over a list of lectures, and not quite in character with the tabular views of prophecies, kings of Israel and Judah, and the Thirty-nine Articles, which did duty elsewhere on the walls, where they were presumed to be studied in spare minutes — which were remarkably spare indeed.

The sporting character of the proprietor of the rooms was further suggested by the huge pair of antlers over the door, bearing on their tines a collection of sticks, whips, and spurs; while, to prove that Mr. Larkyns was not wholly taken up by the charms of the chase, fishing-rods, tandem-whips, cricket-bats, and Joe Mantons, were piled up in odd corners; and single-sticks, boxing-gloves, and foils, gracefully arranged upon the walls, shewed that he occasionally devoted himself to athletic pursuits. An ingenious wire-rack for pipes and meerschaums, and the presence of one or two suspicious-looking boxes, labelled 'collorados,' 'regalia,' 'lukotilla,' and with other unknown words, seemed to intimate that, if Mr. Larkyns was no smoker himself, he at least kept a bountiful supply of 'smoke' for his friends; but the perfumed cloud that was proceeding from his lips as Verdant entered the room, dispelled all doubts on the subject.

He was much changed in appearance during the somewhat long interval since Verdant had last seen him, and his handsome features had assumed a more manly, though perhaps a more rakish look. He was lolling on a couch in the *neglige* attire of dressing-gown and slippers, with his pink striped shirt comfortably open at the neck. Lounging in an easy chair opposite to him was a gentleman clad in tartan-plaid, whose face might only be partially discerned through the glass bottom of a pewter, out of which he was draining the last draught. Between them was a table covered with the ordinary appointments for a breakfast, and the extra-ordinary ones of beer-cup and soda-water. Two Skye terriers, hearing a strange footstep, immediately barked out a challenge of 'Who goes there?' and made Mr. Larkyns aware that an intruder was at hand.

Slightly turning his head, he dimly saw through the smoke a spectacled figure taking off his hat, and holding out an envelope, and without looking further, he said, 'It's no use coming here, young man, and stealing a march in this way! I don't owe *you* any thing; and if I did, it is not convenient to pay it. I told Spavin not to send me any more of his confounded reminders; so go back and tell him that he'll find it all right in the long-run, and that I'm really going to read this term, and shall stump the examiners at last. And now, my friend, you'd better make yourself scarce and vanish! You know where the door lies!'

Our hero was so confounded at this unusual manner of receiving a friend, that he was some little time before he could gasp out, 'Why, Charles Larkyns — don't you remember me? Verdant Green!'

Mr. Larkyns, astonished in his turn, jumped up directly, and came to him with outstretched hands. ''Pon my word, old fellow,' he said, 'I really beg you ten thousand pardons for not recognizing you; but you are so altered — allow me to add, improved, — since I last saw you; you were not a bashaw of two tails, then, you know; and, really, wearing your beaver up, like Hamlet's uncle, I altogether took you for a dun. For I am a victim of a very remarkable monomania. There are in this place wretched beings calling themselves tradesmen, who labour under the impression that I owe them what they facetiously term little bills; and though I have frequently assured their messengers, who are kind enough to come here to inquire for Mr. Larkyns, that that unfortunate gentleman has been obliged to hide himself from persecution in a convent abroad, yet the wretches still hammer at my oak, and disturb my peace of mind. But bring yourself to an anchor, old fellow! This man is Smalls; a capital fellow, whose chief merit consists in his devotion to literature; indeed, he reads so hard that he is called a *fast* man. Smalls! let me introduce my friend Verdant Green, a freshman, — ahem! — and the proprietor, I believe, of your old rooms.'

Our hero made a profound bow to Mr. Smalls, who returned it with great gravity, and said he 'had great pleasure in forming the acquaintance of a freshman like Mr. Verdant Green;' which was doubtless quite true; and he then evinced his devotion to literature by continuing the perusal of one of those vivid and refined accounts of 'a rattling set-to between Nobby Buffer and Hammer Sykes,' for which *Tintinnabulum's Life* is so justly famous.

'I heard from my governor,' said Mr. Larkyns, 'that you were coming up; and in the course of the morning I should have come and looked you up; but the — the fatigues of travelling yesterday,' continued Mr. Larkyns, as a lively recollection of the preceding evening's symposium stole over his mind, 'made me rather later than usual this morning. Have you done any thing in this way?'

Verdant replied that he had breakfasted, although he had not done any thing in the way of cigars, because he never smoked.

'Never smoked! Is it possible!' exclaimed Mr. Smalls, violently interrupting himself in the perusal of *Tintinnabulum's Life*, while some private signals were rapidly telegraphed between him and Mr. Larkyns; 'ah! you'll soon get the better of that weakness! Now, as you're a freshman, you'll perhaps allow me to give you a little advice. The Germans, you know, would never be the deep readers that they are, unless they smoked; and I should advise you to go to the Vice-Chancellor as soon as possible, and ask him for an order for some weeds. He'd be delighted to think you are beginning to set to work so soon!' To which our hero replied, that he was much obliged to Mr. Smalls for his kind advice, and if such were the customs of the place, he should do his best to fulfil them.

'Perhaps you'll be surprised at our simple repast, Verdant,' said Mr. Larkyns; 'but it's our misfortune. It all comes of hard reading and late hours: the midnight oil, you know, must be supplied, and *will* be paid for; the nervous system gets strained to excess, and you have to call in the doctor. Well, what does he do? Why, he prescribes a regular course of tonics; and I flatter myself that I am a very docile patient, and take my bitter beer regularly, and without complaining.' In proof of which Mr. Charles Larkyns took a long pull at the pewter.

'But you know, Larkyns,' observed Mr. Smalls, 'that was nothing to my case, when I got laid up with elephantiasis on the biceps of the lungs, and had a fur coat in my stomach!'

'Dear me!' said Verdant sympathizingly; 'and was that also through too much study?'

'Why, of course!' replied Mr. Smalls; 'it couldn't have been anything else — from the symptoms, you know! But then the sweets of learning surpass the bitters. Talk of the plea-sures of the dead languages, indeed! why, how many jolly nights have you and I, Larkyns, passed 'down among the dead men!''

Charles Larkyns had just been looking over the letter which Verdant had brought him, and said, 'The governor writes that you'd like me to put you up to the ways of the place, because they are fresh to you, and you are fresh (ahem! very!) to them. Now, I am going to wine with Smalls to-night, to meet a few nice, quiet, hard-working men (eh, Smalls?), and I daresay Smalls will do the civil, and ask you also.'

'Certainly!' said Mr. Smalls, who saw a prospect of amusement, 'delighted, I assure you! I hope to see you — after Hall, you know, — but I hope you don't object to a very quiet party?'

'Oh, dear no!' replied Verdant; 'I much prefer a quiet party; indeed, I have always been used to quiet parties; and I shall be very glad to come.'

'Well, that's settled then,' said Charles Larkyns; 'and, in the mean time, Verdant, let us take a prowl about the old place, and I'll put you up to a thing or two, and shew you some of the freshman's sights. But you must go and get your cap and gown, old fellow, and then by that time I'll be ready for you.'

Whether there are really any sights in Oxford that are more especially devoted, or adapted, to its freshmen, we will not undertake to affirm; but if there are, they could not have had a better expositor than Mr. Charles Larkyns, or a more credible visitor than Mr. Verdant Green. His credibility was rather strongly put to the test as they turned into the High Street, when his companion directed his attention to an individual on the opposite side of the street, with a voluminous gown, and enormous cocked hat profusely adorned with gold lace. 'I suppose you know who that is, Verdant? No! Why, that's the Bishop of Oxford! Ah, I see, he's a very different-looking man to what you had expected; but then these university robes so change the appearance. That is his official dress, as the Visitor of the Ashmolean!'

Mr. Verdant Green having 'swallowed' this, his friend was thereby enabled, not only to use up old 'sells,' but also to draw largely on his invention for new ones. Just then, there came along the street, walking in a sort of young procession, — the Vice-Chancellor, with his Esquire and Yeoman-bedels. The silver maces, carried by these latter gentlemen, made them by far the most showy part of the procession, and accordingly Mr. Larkyns seized the favourable opportunity to point out the foremost bedel, and say, 'You see that man with the poker and loose cap? Well, that's the Vice-Chancellor.'

'But what does he walk in procession for?' inquired our freshman.

'Ah, poor man!' said Mr. Larkyns, 'he's obliged to do it.' 'Uneasy lies the head that wears a crown,' you know; and he can never go anywhere, or do anything, without carrying that poker, and having the other minor pokers to follow him. They never leave him, not even at night. Two of the pokers stand on each side his bed, and relieve each other every two hours. So, I need hardly say, that he is obliged to be a bachelor.'

'It must be a very wearisome office,' remarked our freshman, who fully believed all that was told to him.

'Wearisome, indeed; and that's the reason why they are obliged to change the Vice-Chancellors so often. It would kill most people, only they are always selected for their strength, — and height,' he added, as a brilliant idea just struck him.

They had turned down Magpie Lane, and so by Oriel College, where one of the fire-plug notices had caught Mr. Larkyns' eye. 'You see that,' he said; 'well, that's one of the plates they put up to record the Vice's height. F.P. 7 feet, you see: the initials of his name, — Frederick Plumptre!'

'He scarcely seemed so tall as that,' said our hero, 'though certainly a tall man. But the gown makes a difference, I suppose.'

'His height was a very lucky thing for him, however,' continued Mr. Larkyns; 'I dare say when you have heard that it was only those who stood high in the University that were elected to rule it, you little thought of the true meaning of the term?'

'I certainly never did,' said the freshman, innocently; 'but I knew that the customs of Oxford must of course be very different from those of other places.'

'Yes, you'll soon find that out,' replied Mr. Larkyns, meaningly. 'But here we are at Merton, whose Merton ale is as celebrated as Burton ale. You see the man giving in the letters to the porter? Well, he's one of their principal men. Each college does its own postal department; and at Merton there are fourteen postmasters, for they get no end of letters there.'

'Oh, yes!' said our hero, 'I remember Mr. Larkyns, — your father, the rector, I mean, — telling us that the son of one of his old friends had been a postmaster of Merton; but I fancied that he had said it had something to do with a scholarship.'

'Ah, you see, it's a long while since the governor was here, and his memory fails him,' remarked Mr. Charles Larkyns, very unfilially. 'Let us turn down the Merton fields, and round into St. Aldate's. We may perhaps be in time to see the Vice come down to Christ Church.'

'What does he go there for?' asked Mr. Verdant Green.

'To wind up the great clock, and put big Tom in order. Tom is the bell that you hear at nine each night; the Vice has to see that he is in proper condition, and, as you have seen, goes out with his pokers for that purpose.'

On their way, Charles Larkyns pointed out, close to Folly Bridge, a house profusely decorated with figures and indescribable ornaments, which he informed our freshman was Blackfriars' Hall, where all the men who had been once plucked were obliged to migrate to; and that Folly Bridge received its name from its propinquity to the Hall. They were too late to see the Vice-Chancellor wind up the clock of Christ Church; but as they passed by the college, they met two gownsmen who recognized Mr. Larkyns by a slight nod. 'Those are two Christ Church men,' he said, 'and noblemen. The one with the Skye-terrier's coat and eye-glass is the Earl of Whitechapel, the Duke of Minories' son. I dare say you know the other man. No! Why, he is Lord Thomas Peeper, eldest son of the Lord Godiva who hunts our county. I knew him in the field.'

'But why do they wear *gold* tassels to their caps?' inquired the freshman.

'Ah,' said the ingenious Mr. Larkyns, shaking his head; 'I had rather you'd not have asked me that question, because that's the disgraceful part of the business. But these lords, you see, they *will* live at a faster pace than us commoners, who can't stand a champagne breakfast above once a term or so. Why, those gold tassels are the badges of drunkenness!'

'Of drunkenness! dear me!'

'Yes, it's very sad, isn't it?' pursued Mr. Larkyns; 'and I wonder that Peeper in particular should give way to such things. But you see how they brazen it out, and walk about as coolly as though nothing had happened. It's just the same sort of punishment,' continued Mr. Larkyns, whose inventive powers increased with the demand that the freshman's gullibility imposed upon them, — 'it is just the same sort of thing that they do with the Greenwich pensioners. When *they* have been trangressing the laws of sobriety, you know, they are made marked men by having to wear a yellow coat as a punishment; and our dons borrowed the idea, and made yellow tassels the badges of intoxication. But for the credit of the University, I'm glad to say that you'll not find many men so disgraced.'

They now turned down the New Road, and came to a strongly castellated building, which Mr. Larkyns pointed out (and truly) as Oxford Castle or the Gaol; and he added (untruly), 'if you hear Botany-Bay College spoken of, this is the place that's meant. It's a delicate way of referring to the temporary sojourn that any undergrad has been forced to make there, to say that he belongs to Botany-Bay College.'

They now turned back, up Queen Street and High Street, when, as they were passing All Saints, Mr. Larkyns pointed out a pale, intellectual looking man who passed them, and said, 'That man is Cram, the patent safety. He's the first coach in Oxford.'

'A coach!' said our freshman, in some wonder.

'Oh, I forgot you didn't know college-slang. I suppose a royal mail is the only gentleman coach that *you* know of. Why, in Oxford, a coach means a private tutor, you must know; and those who can't afford a coach, get a cab, — *alias* a crib, — *alias* a translation. You see, Verdant, you are gradually being initiated into Oxford mysteries.'

'I am, indeed,' said our hero, to whom a new world was opening.

They had now turned round by the west

end of St. Mary's, and were passing Brasenose; and Mr. Larkyns drew Verdant's attention to the brazen nose that is such a conspicuous object over the entrance-gate.

'That,' said he, 'was modelled from a cast of the Principal feature of the first Head of the college; and so the college was named Brazen-nose. The nose was formerly used as a place of punishment for any misbehaving Brazennosian, who had to sit upon it for two hours, and was not *countenanced* until he had done so. These punishments were so frequent that they gradually wore down the nose to its present small dimensions.

'This round building,' continued Mr. Larkyns, pointing to the Radcliffe, 'is the Vice-Chancellor's house. He has to go each night up to that balcony on the top, and look round to see if all's safe. Those heads,' he said, as they passed the Ashmolean, 'are supposed to be the twelve Caesars; only there happen, I believe, to be thirteen of them. I think that they are the busts of the original Heads of Houses.'

Mr. Larkyns' inventive powers having been now somewhat exhausted, he proposed that they should go back to Brazenface and have some lunch. This they did; after which Mr. Verdant Green wrote to his mother a long account of his friend's kindness, and the trouble he had taken to explain the most interesting sights that could be seen by a Freshman.

'Are you writing to your governor, Verdant?' asked the friend, who had made his way to our hero's rooms, and was now perfuming them with a little tobacco-smoke.

'No; I am writing to my mama — mother, I mean!'

'Oh! to the missis!' was the reply; 'that's just the same. Well, had you not better take the opportunity to ask them to send you a proper certificate that you have been vaccinated, and had the measles favourably?'

'But what is that for?' inquired our Freshman, always anxious to learn. 'Your father sent up the certificate of my baptism, and I thought that was the only one wanted.'

'Oh,' said Mr. Charles Larkyns, 'they give you no end of trouble at these places; and they require the vaccination certificate before you go in for your responsions, — the Little-go, you know. You need not mention my name in your letter as having told you this. It will be quite enough to say that you understand such a thing is required.'

Verdant accordingly penned the request; and Charles Larkyns smoked on, and thought his friend the very beau-ideal of a Freshman. 'By the way, Verdant,' he said, desirous not to lose any opportunity, 'you are going to wine with Smalls this evening; and, — excuse me mentioning it, — but I suppose you would go properly dressed, — white tie, kids, and that sort of thing, eh? Well! ta, ta, till then. 'We meet again at Philippi!''

Acting upon the hint thus given, our hero, when Hall was over made himself uncommonly spruce in a new white tie, and spotless kids; and as he was dressing, drew a mental picture of the party to which he was going. It was to be composed of quiet, steady men, who were such hard readers as to be called 'fast men.' He should therefore hear some delightful and rational conversation on the literature of ancient Greece and Rome, the present standard of scholarship in the University, speculations on the forthcoming prize-poems, comparisons between various expectant class-men, and delightful topics of a kindred nature; and the evening would be passed in a grave and sedate manner; and after a couple of glasses of wine had been leisurely sipped, they should have a very enjoyable tea, and would separate for an early rest, mutually gratified and improved.

This was the nature of Mr. Verdant Green's speculations; but whether they were realized or no, may be judged by transferring the scene a few hours later to Mr. Smalls' room.

8

Mr. Verdant Green's Morning Reflections are Not So Pleasant as his Evening Diversions

Mr. Smalls' room was filled with smoke and noise. Supper had been cleared away; the glasses were now sparkling on the board, and the wine was ruby bright. The table, moreover, was supplied with spirituous liquors and mixtures of all descriptions, together with many varieties of 'cup,' — a cup which not only cheers, but occasionally inebriates; and this miscellany of liquids was now being drunk on the premises by some score and a half of gentlemen, who were sitting round the table, and standing or lounging about in various parts of the room. Heading the table, sat the host, loosely attired in a neat dressing gown of crimson and blue, in an attitude which allowed him to swing his legs easily, if not gracefully, over the arm of his chair, and to converse cheerfully with Charles Larkyns, who was leaning over the chair-back. Visible to the naked eye, on Mr. Smalls' left hand, appeared the white tie and full evening dress which decorated the person of Mr. Verdant Green.

A great consumption of tobacco was going on, not only through the medium of cigars, but also of meerschaums, short 'dhudheens' of envied colour, and the genuine yard of clay; and Verdant, while he was scarcely aware of what he was doing, found himself, to his great amazement, with a real cigar in his mouth, which he was industriously sucking, and with great difficulty keeping alight. Our hero felt that the unexpected exigencies of the case demanded from him some sacrifice; while he consoled himself by the reflection, that, on the homoeopathic principle of 'likes cure likes,' a cigar was the best preventive against any ill effects arising from the combination of the thirty gentlemen who were generating smoke with all the ardour of lime-kilns or young volcanoes, and filling Mr. Smalls' small room with an atmosphere that was of the smoke, smoky. Smoke produces thirst; and the cup, punch, egg-flip, sherry-cobblers, and other liquids, which had been so liberally provided, were being consumed by the members of the party as though it had been their drink from childhood; while the conversation was of a kind very different to what our hero had anticipated, being for the most part vapid and unmeaning, and (must it

be confessed?) occasionally too highly fla-
voured with improprieties for it to be
faithfully recorded in these pages of most
perfect propriety.

The literature of ancient Greece and
Rome was not even referred to; and when
Verdant, who, from the unusual combination
of the smoke and liquids, was beginning to
feel extremely amiable and talkative, —
made a reflective observation (addressed to
the company generally) which sounded like
the words 'Nunc vino pellite curas, Cras
ingens,' — he was immediately interrupted
by the voice of Mr. Bouncer, crying out,
'Who's that talking shop about engines?
Holloa, Gig-lamps!' — Mr. Bouncer, it must
be observed, had facetiously adopted the
sobriquet which had been bestowed on
Verdant and his spectacles on their first
appearance outside the Oxford coach, —
'Holloa, Gig-lamps, is that you ill-treating
the dead languages? I'm ashamed of you! a
venerable party like you ought to be above
such things. There! don't blush, old feller,
but give us a song! It's the punishment for
talking shop, you know.'

There was an immediate hammering of
tables and jingling of glasses, accompanied
with loud cries of 'Mr. Green for a song! Mr.
Green! Mr. Gig-lamps' song!' cries which

110

nearly brought our hero to the verge of idiotcy.

Charles Larkyns saw this, and came to the rescue. 'Gentlemen,' he said, addressing the company, 'I know that my friend Verdant *can* sing, and that, like a good bird, he *will* sing. But while he is mentally looking over his numerous stock of songs, and selecting one for our amusement, I beg to fill up our valuable time, by asking you to fill up a bumper to the health of our esteemed host Smalls (*vociferous cheers*) — a man whose private worth is only to be equalled by the purity of his milk-punch and the excellence of his weeds (*hear hear*). Bumpers, gentlemen, and no heel-taps! and though I am sorry to interfere with Mr. Fosbrooke's private enjoyments, yet I must beg to suggest to him that he has been so much engaged in drowning his personal cares in the bowl over which he is so skilfully presiding, that my glass has been allowed to sparkle on the board empty and useless.' And as Charles Larkyns held out his glass towards Mr. Fosbrooke and the punch-bowl, he trolled out, in a rich, manly voice, old Cowley's anacreontic:

'Fill up the bowl then, fill it high!
Fill all the glasses there! For why
Should every creature drink but I?

Why, man of morals, tell me why?'

By the time that the 'man of morals' had ladled out for the company, and that Mr. Smalls' health had been drunk and responded to amid uproarious applause, Charles Larkyns' friendly diversion in our hero's favour had succeeded, and Mr. Verdant Green had regained his confidence, and had decided upon one of those vocal efforts which, in the bosom of his own family, and to the pianoforte accompaniment of his sisters, was accustomed to meet with great applause. And when he had hastily tossed off another glass of milk-punch (merely to clear his throat), he felt bold enough to answer the spirit-rappings which were again demanding 'Mr. Green's song!' It was given much in the following manner:

Mr. Verdant Green (in low plaintive tones, and fresh alarm at hearing the sounds of his own voice). 'I dreamt that I dwe-elt in mar-arble halls, with' —
Mr. Bouncer (interrupting). 'Spit it out, Gig-lamps! Dis child can't hear whether it's Maudlin Hall you're singing about, or what.'
Omnes. 'Order! or-*der*! Shut up, Bouncer!'
Charles Larkyns (encouragingly). 'Try back, Verdant: never mind.'
Mr. Verdant Green (tries back, with increased

112

confusion of ideas, resulting principally from the milk-punch and tobacco). 'I dreamt that I dwe-elt in mar-arble halls, with vassals and serfs at my si-hi-hide; and — and — I beg your pardon, gentlemen, I really forget — oh, I know! — and I also dre-eamt, which ple-eased me most — no, that's not it' —

Mr. Bouncer (who does not particularly care for the words of a song, but only appreciates the chorus) — 'That'll do, old feller! We ain't pertickler,-*(rushes with great deliberation and noise to the chorus)* 'That you lo-oved me sti-ill the sa-ha-hame — chorus, gentlemen!'

Omnes (in various keys and time). 'That you lo-oved me sti-ill the same.'

Mr. Bouncer (to Mr. Green, alluding remotely to the opera). 'Now my Bohemian gal, can't you come out to-night? Spit us out a yard or two more, Gig-lamps.'

Mr. Verdant Green (who has again taken the opportunity to clear his throat). 'I dreamt that I dwe-elt in mar-arble- no! I beg pardon! sang that *(desperately)* — that sui-uitors sou-ught my hand, that knights on their *(hic)* ben-ended kne-e-ee — had *(hic)* riches too gre-eat to' — *(Mr. Verdant Green smiles benignantly upon the company)* — 'Don't ree'lect anymo.'

Mr. Bouncer (who is not to be defrauded of the chorus). 'Chorus, gentlemen! —That you'll lo-ove me sti-ill the sa-a-hame!'
Omnes (ad libitum). 'That you'll lo-ove me sti-ill the same!'

Though our hero had ceased to sing, he was still continuing to clear his throat by the aid of the milk-punch, and was again industriously sucking his cigar, which he had not yet succeeded in getting half through, although he had re-lighted it about twenty times. All this was observed by the watchful eyes of Mr. Bouncer, who, whispering to his neighbour, and bestowing a distributive wink on the company generally, rose and made the following remarks:-

'Mr. Smalls, and gents all: I don't often get on my pins to trouble you with a neat and appropriate speech; but on an occasion like the present, when we are honoured with the presence of a party who has just delighted us with what I may call a flood of harmony *(hear, hear)*, — and has pitched it so uncommon strong in the vocal line, as to considerably take the shine out of the woodpecker-tapping, that we've read of in the pages of history *(hear, hear: 'Go it again, Bouncer!')*, — when, gentlemen, I see before me this old original Little Wobbler, — need I say that I allude to Mr. Verdant Green? — (*vociferous cheers*)-I feel it a sort of, what you call a privilege, d'ye see, to stand on my pins, and propose that respected party's jolly good health (*renewed cheers*). Mr. Verdant Green, gentlemen, has but lately come among us, and is, in point of fact, what you call a freshman; but, gentlemen, we've already seen enough of him to feel aware that — that Brazenface has gained an acquisition, which — which — (*cries of 'Tally-ho! Yoicks! Hark forrud!'*) Exactly so, gentlemen: so, as I see you are all anxious to do honour to our freshman, I beg, without further preface, to give you the health of Mr. Verdant Green! With all the honours. Chorus, gents!

'For he's a jolly good fellow!
For he's a jolly good fellow!!
For he's a jolly good f-e-e-ell-ow!!!
        Which nobody can deny!'

This chorus was taken up and prolonged in the most indefinite manner; little Mr. Bouncer fairly revelling in it, and only regretting that he had not his post-horn with him to further contribute to the harmony of the evening. It seemed to be a great art in the singers of the chorus to dwell as long as possible on the third repetition of the word 'fellow,' and in the most defiant manner to pounce down on the bold affirmation by which it is followed; and then to lyrically proclaim that, not only was it a way they had in the Varsity to drive dull care away, but that the same practice was also pursued in the army and navy for the attainment of a similar end.

When the chorus had been sung over three or four times, and Mr. Verdant Green's name had been proclaimed with equal noise, that gentleman rose (with great difficulty), to return thanks. He was understood to speak as follows:

'Genelum anladies (*cheers*), — I meangenelum. (*'That's about the ticket, old feller!' from Mr. Bouncer.*) Customd syam plic speakn, I — I — (*hear, hear*) — feel bliged drinkmyel. I'm fresman, genelum, and prowtitle (*loud cheers*). Myfren Misserboucer, fallowme callm myfren! (*'In course, Gig-lamps, you do me proud, old feller.'*) Myfren Misserboucer seszime fresman — prow title, sureyou (*hear, hear*). Genelmun, werall jolgoodfles, anwe wogohotillmorrin! (*'We won't, we won't! not a bit of it!'*) Gelmul, I'm fresmal, an namesgreel, gelmul (*cheers*). Fanyul dousmewor, herescardinpock'lltellm! Misser Verdalgreel, Braseface, Oxul fresmal, anprowtitle! (*Great cheering and rattling of glasses, during which Mr. Verdant Green's coat-tails are made the receptacles for empty bottles, lobsters' claws, and other miscellaneous articles.*) Misserboucer said was fresmal. If Misserboucer wantsultme ('*No, no!*'), herescardinpock'lltellm namesverdalgreel, Braseface! Not shameofit-gelmul! prowtitle! (*Great applause.*) I doewaltilsul Misserboucer! thenwhysee sultme? thaswaw Iwaltknow! (*Loud cheers, and roars of laughter, in which Mr. Verdant Green suddenly joins to the best of his ability.*) I'm anoxful fresmal, gelmul, 'fmyfrel Misserboucer loume-callimso. (*Cheers and laughter, in which Mr. Verdant Green feebly joins.*) Anweerall jol-goodfles, anwe wogohotilmorril, an I'm fresmal, gelmul, anfanyul dowsmewor — an I — doe-feel quiwell!'

This was the termination of Mr. Verdant Green's speech, for after making a few unintelligible sounds, his knees suddenly gave way, and with a benevolent smile he disappeared beneath the table.

★ ★ ★

Half an hour afterwards two gentlemen might have been seen, bearing with staggering steps across the moonlit quad the huddled form of a third gentleman, who was clothed in full evening dress, and appeared incapable of taking care of himself. The two first gentlemen set down their burden under an open doorway, painted over with a large 4; and then, by pulling and pushing, assisted it to guide its steps up a narrow and intricate staircase, until they had gained the third floor, and stood before a door, over which the moonlight revealed, in newly-painted white letters, the name of 'MR. VERDANT GREEN.'

'Well, old feller,' said the first gentleman, 'how do you feel now, after 'Sich a getting up stairs'?'

'Feel much berrer now,' said their late burden; 'feel quite-comfurble! Shallgotobed!'

'Well, Gig-lamps,' said the first speaker, 'and By-by won't be at all a bad move for you. D'ye think you can unrig yourself and get between the sheets, eh, my beauty?'

'Its allri, allri!' was the reply; 'limycandle!'

'No, no,' said the second gentleman, as he pulled up the window-blind, and let in the moonlight; 'here's quite as much light as you want. It's almost morning.'

'Sotis,' said the gentleman in the evening costume: 'anlittlebirds beginsingsoon! I like littlebirds sing! jollittlebirds!' The speaker had suddenly fallen upon his bed, and was lying thereon at full length, with his feet on the pillow.

'He'll be best left in this way,' said the

second speaker, as he removed the pillow to the proper place, and raised the prostrate gentleman's head; 'I'll take off his choker and make him easy about the neck, and then we'll shut him up, and leave him. Why the beggar's asleep already!' And so the two gentlemen went away, and left him safe and sleeping.

It is conjectured, however, that he must have got up shortly after this, and finding himself with his clothes on, must have considered that a lighted candle was indispensably necessary to undress by; for when Mrs. Tester came at her usual early hour to light the fires and prepare the sitting-rooms, she discovered him lying on the carpet embracing the coal-skuttle, with a candle by his side. The good woman raised him, and did not leave him until she had, in the most motherly manner, safely tucked him up in bed.

★ ★ ★

Clink, clank! clink, clank! tingle, tangle! tingle, tangle! Are demons smiting ringing hammers into Mr. Verdant Green's brain, or is the dreadful bell summoning him to rise for morning chapel?

Mr. Filcher puts an end to the doubt by putting his head in at the bedroom door, and saying, 'Time for chapel, sir! Chapel,' thought Mr. Filcher; 'here is a chap ill, indeed! — Bain't you well, sir? Restless you look!'

Oh, the shame and agony that Mr. Verdant Green felt! The desire to bury his head under the clothes, away from Robert's and everyone else's sight; the fever that throbbed his brain and parched his lips, and made him long to drink up Ocean; the eyes that felt like burning lead; the powerless hands that trembled like a weak old man's; the voice that came in faltering tones that jarred the brain at every word! How he despised himself; how he loathed the very idea of wine; how he resolved never, never to transgress so again! But perhaps Mr. Verdant Green was not the only Oxford freshman who has made this resolution.

'Bain't you well, sir?' repeated Mr. Filcher, with a passing thought that freshmen were sadly degenerating, and could not manage their three bottles as they did when he was first a scout: 'bain't you well, sir?'

'Not very well, Robert, thank you. I — my head aches, and I'm afraid I shall not be able to get up for chapel. Will the Master be very angry?'

'Well, he *might* be, you see, sir,' replied Mr. Filcher, who never lost an opportunity of making anything out of his master's infirmities; 'but if you'll leave it to me, sir, I'll make it all right for you, *I* will. Of course you'd like to take out an *aeger*, sir; and I can bring you your Commons just the same. Will that do, sir?'

'Oh, thank you; yes, any thing. You will find five shillings in my waistcoat-pocket, Robert; please to take it; but I can't eat.'

'Thank'ee, sir,' said the scout, as he abstracted the five shillings; 'but you'd better have a bit of somethin', sir; — a cup of strong tea, or somethin'. Mr. Smalls, sir, when he were pleasant, he always had beer, sir; but p'raps you ain't been used to bein' pleasant, sir, and slops might suit you better, sir.'

'Oh, any thing, any thing!' groaned our poor, unheroic hero, as he turned his face to the wall, and endeavoured to recollect in what way he had been 'pleasant' the night before. But, alas! the wells of his memory had, for the time, been poisoned, and nothing clear or pure could be drawn therefrom. So he got up and looked at himself in the glass, and scarcely recognized the tangled-haired, sallow-faced wretch, whose bloodshot eyes gazed heavily at him from the mirror. So he nervously drained the water-bottle, and buried himself once more among the tossed and tumbled bed-clothes.

The tea really did him some good, and enabled him to recover sufficient nerve to go feebly through the operation of dressing; though it was lucky that nature had not yet brought Mr. Verdant Green to the necessity of shaving, for the handling of a razor might have been attended with suicidal results, and have brought these veracious memoirs and their hero to an untimely end.

He had just sat down to a second edition of tea, and was reading a letter that the post had brought him from his sister Mary, in which she said, 'I dare say by this time you have found Mr. Charles Larkyns a very *delightful* companion, and I *am sure* a very *valuable* one; as, from what the rector says, he appears to be so *steady*, and has such *nice quiet* companions:' — our hero had read as far as this, when a great noise just without his door, caused the letter to drop from his trembling hands; and, between loud *fanfares* from a post-horn, and heavy thumps upon the oak, a voice was heard, demanding 'Entrance in the Proctor's name.'

Mr. Verdant Green had for the first time 'sported his oak.' Under any circumstances it would have been a mere form, since his bashful politeness would have induced him to open it to any comer; but, at the dreaded name of the Proctor, he sprang from his chair, and while impositions, rustications, and expulsions rushed tumultuously through his disordered brain, he nervously undid the springlock, and admitted — not the Proctor, but the 'steady' Mr. Charles Larkyns and his 'nice quiet companion,' little Mr. Bouncer, who testified his joy at the success of their *coup d'etat*, by blowing on his horn loud blasts that might have been borne by Fontarabian echoes, and which rang through poor Verdant's head with indescribable jarrings.

'Well, Verdant,' said Charles Larkyns, 'how do you find yourself this morning? You look rather shaky.'

'He ain't a very lively picter, is he?' remarked little Mr. Bouncer, with the air of a connoisseur; 'peakyish you feel, don't you, now, with a touch of the mulligrubs in your collywobbles? Ah, I know what it is, my boy.'

It was more than our hero did; and he could only reply that he did not feel very well. 'I — I had a glass of claret after some lobster-salad, and I think it disagreed with me.'

'Not a doubt of it, Verdant,' said Charles Larkyns very gravely; 'it would have precisely the same effect that the salmon always has at a public dinner, — bring on great hilarity, succeeded by a pleasing delirium, and concluding in a horizontal position, and a demand for soda-water.'

'I hope,' said our hero, rather faintly, 'that I did not conduct myself in an unbecoming manner last night; for I am sorry to say that I do not remember all that occurred.'

'I should think not, Gig-lamps, You were as drunk as a besom,' said little Mr. Bouncer, with a side wink to Mr. Larkyns, to prepare that gentleman for what was to follow. 'Why, you got on pretty well till old Slowcoach came in, and then you certainly did go it, and no mistake!'

'Mr. Slowcoach!' groaned the freshman. 'Good gracious! is it possible that *he* saw me? I don't remember it.'

'And it would be lucky for you if *he* didn't,' replied Mr, Bouncer. 'Why his rooms, you know, are in the same angle of the quad as Smalls'; so, when you came to shy the empty bottles out of Smalls' window at *his* window — '

'Shy empty bottles! Oh!' gasped the freshman.

'Why, of course, you see, he couldn't stand that sort of game — it wasn't to be expected; so he puts his head out of the bedroom window — and then, don't you remember crying out, as you pointed to the tassel of his night-cap sticking up straight on end, 'Tally-ho! Unearth'd at last! Look at his brush!' Don't you remember that, Gig-lamps?'

'Oh, oh, no!' groaned Mr. Bouncer's victim: 'I can't remember, — oh, what *could* have induced me!'

'By Jove, you *must* have been screwed! Then I daresay you don't remember wanting to have a polka with him, when he came up to Smalls' rooms?'

'A polka! Oh dear! Oh no! Oh!'

'Or asking him if his mother knew he was out, — and what he'd take for his cap without the tassel; and telling him that he was the joy of your heart, — and that you should never be happy unless he'd smile as he was wont to smile, and would love you then as now, — and saying all sorts of bosh? What, not remember it! 'Oh, what a noble mind is here o'erthrown!' as some cove says in Shakespeare. But how screwed you *must* have been, Gig-lamps!'

'And do you think,' inquired our hero, after a short but sufficiently painful reflection, — 'do you think that Mr. Slowcoach will — oh! — expel me?'

'Why, it's rather a shave for it,' replied his tormentor; 'but the best thing you can do is to write an apology at once: pitch it pretty strong in the pathetic line, — say it's your first offence, and that you'll never be a naughty boy again, and all that sort of thing. You just do that, Gig-lamps, and I'll see that the note goes to — the proper place.'

'Oh, thank you!' said the freshman; and while, with equal difficulty from agitation both of mind and body, he composed and penned the note, Mr. Bouncer ordered up some buttery beer, and Charles Larkyns prepared some soda-water with a dash of brandy, which he gave Verdant to drink, and which considerably refreshed that gentleman.

'And I should advise you,' he said, 'to go out for a constitutional; for walking-time's come, although you have but just done your breakfast. A blow up Headington Hill will do you good, and set you on your legs again.'

So Verdant, after delivering up his note to Mr. Bouncer, took his friend's advice, and set out for his constitutional in his cap and gown, feeling afraid to move without them, lest he should thereby trespass some law. This, of course, gained him some attention after he had crossed Magdalen Bridge; and he might have almost been taken for the original of that impossible gownsman who appears in Turner's well-known 'View of Oxford, from Ferry Hincksey,' as wandering.

'Remote, unfriended, solitary, *slow*,' —

in a corn-field, in the company of an umbrella!

Among the many pedestrians and equestrians that he encountered, our freshman espied a short and very stout gentleman, whose shovel-hat, short apron, and general decanical costume, proclaimed him to be a don of some importance. He was riding a pad-nag, who ambled placidly along, without so much as hinting at an outbreak into a canter; a performance that, as it seemed, might have been attended with disastrous consequences to his rider. Our hero noticed, that the trio of undergraduates who were walking before him, while they passed others, who were evidently dons, without the slightest notice (being in mufti), yet not only raised their hats to the stout gentleman, but also separated for that purpose, and performed the salute at intervals of about ten yards. And he further remarked, that while the stout gentleman appeared to be exceedingly gratified at the notice he received, yet that he had also very great difficulty in returning the rapid salutations; and only accomplished them and retained his seat by catching at the pommel of his saddle, or the mane of his steed, — a proceeding which the pad-nag seemed perfectly used to.

Mr. Verdant Green returned home from his walk, feeling all the better for the fresh air and change of scene; but he still looked, as his neighbour, Mr. Bouncer, kindly informed him, 'uncommon seedy, and doosid fishy about the eyes;' and it was some days even before he had quite recovered from the novel excitement of Mr. Smalls' 'quiet party.'

9

Mr. Verdant Green Attends Lectures, and, in Despite of Sermons, has Dealings with Filthy Lucre

Our freshman, like all other freshmen, now began to think seriously of work, and plunged desperately into all the lectures that it was possible for him to attend, beginning every course with a zealousness that shewed him to be filled with the idea that such a plan was eminently necessary for the attainment of his degree; in all this in every respect deserving the Humane Society's medal for his brave plunge into the depths of the Pierian spring, to fish up the beauties that had been immersed therein by the poets of old. When we say that our freshman, like other freshmen, 'began' this course, we use the verb advisedly; for, like many other freshmen who start with a burst in learning's race, he soon got winded, and fell back among the ruck. But the course of lectures, like the course of true love, will not always run smooth, even to those who undertake it with the same courage as Mr. Verdant Green.

The dryness of the daily routine of lectures, which varied about as much as the steak-and-chop, chop-and-steak dinners of ancient taverns, was occasionally relieved by episodes, which, though not witty in themselves, were yet the cause of wit in others; for it takes but little to cause amusement in a lecture-room, where a bad construe; or the imaginative excuses of late-comers; or the confusion of some young gentleman who has to turn over the leaf of his Greek play and finds it uncut; or the pounding of the same gentleman in the middle of the first chorus; or his offensive extrication therefrom through the medium of some Cumberland barbarian; or the officiousness of the same barbarian to pursue the lecture when every one else has, with singular unanimity, 'read no further;' — all these circumstances, although perhaps dull enough in themselves, are nevertheless productive of some mirth in a lecture-room.

But if there were often late-comers to the lectures, there were occasionally early-goers from them. Had Mr. Four-in-hand Fosbrooke an engagement to ride his horse *Tearaway* in the amateur steeple-chase, and was he constrained, by circumstances over which (as he protested) he had no control, to put in a regular appearance at Mr. Slowcoach's lectures, what was it necessary for him to do more than to come to lecture in a long greatcoat, put his handkerchief to his face as though his nose were bleeding, look appealingly at Mr. Slowcoach, and, as he made his exit, pull aside the long greatcoat, and display to his admiring colleagues the snowy cords and tops that would soon be pressing against *Tearaway's* sides, that gallant animal being then in waiting, with its trusty groom, in the alley at the back of Brazenface? And if little Mr. Bouncer, for astute reasons of his own, wished Mr. Slowcoach to believe that he (Mr. B.) was particularly struck with his (Mr. S.'s) remarks on the force of *kata* in composition, what was to prevent Mr. Bouncer from feigning to make a note of these remarks by the aid of a cigar instead of an ordinary pencil?

But besides the regular lectures of Mr. Slowcoach, our hero had also the privilege of attending those of the Rev. Richard Harmony. Much learning, though it had not made Mr. Harmony mad, had, at least in conjunction with his natural tendencies, contributed to make him extremely eccentric; while to much perusal of Greek and Hebrew MSS., he probably owed his defective vision. These infirmities, instead of being regarded with sympathy, as wounds received by Mr. Harmony in the classical engagements in the

131

various fields of literature, were, to Mr. Verdant Green's surprise, much imposed upon; for it was a favourite pastime with the gentlemen who attended Mr. Harmony's lectures, to gradually raise up the lecture-table by a concerted action, and when Mr. Harmony's book had nearly reached to the level of his nose, to then suddenly drop the table to its original level; upon which Mr. Harmony, to the immense gratification of all concerned, would rub his eyes, wipe his glasses, and murmur, 'Dear me! dear me! how my head swims this morning!' And then he would perhaps ring for his servant, and order his usual remedy, an orange, at which he would suck abstractedly, nor discover any difference in the flavour even when a lemon was surreptitiously substituted. And thus he would go on through the lecture, sucking his orange (or lemon), explaining and expounding in the most skilful and lucid manner, and yet, as far as the 'table-movement' was concerned, as unsuspecting and as witless as a little child.

Mr. Verdant Green not only (at first) attended lectures with exemplary diligence and regularity, but he also duly went to morning and evening chapel; nor, when Sundays came, did he neglect to turn his feet towards St. Mary's to hear the University sermons. Their effect was as striking to him as it probably is to most persons who have only been accustomed to the usual services of country churches. First, there was the peculiar character of the congregation: down below, the vice-chancellor in his throne, overlooking the other dons in their stalls (being 'a complete realization of stalled Oxon!' as Charles Larkyns whispered to our hero), who were relieved in colour by their crimson or scarlet hoods; and then, 'upstairs,' in the north and the great west galleries, the black mass of undergraduates; while a few ladies' bonnets and heads of male visitors peeped from the pews in the aisles, or looked out from the curtains of the organ-gallery, where, 'by the kind permission of Dr. Elvey,' they were accommodated with seats, and watched with wonder, while

'The wild wizard's fingers,
With magical skill,
Made music that lingers
In memory still.'

Then there was the bidding-prayer, in which Mr. Verdant Green was somewhat astonished to hear the long list of founders and benefactors, 'such as were, Philip Pluckton, Bishop of Iffley; King Edward the Seventh;

133

Stephen de Henley, Earl of Bagley, and Maud his wife; Nuneham Courtney, knight,' with a long et-cetera; though, as the preacher happened to be a Brazenface man, our hero found that he was 'most chiefly bound to praise Clement Abingdon, Bishop of Jericho, and founder of the college of Brazenface; Richard Glover, Duke of Woodstock; Giles Peckwater, Abbot of Beney; and Binsey Green, Doctor of Music; — benefactors of the same.'

Then there was the sermon itself; the abstrusely learned and classical character of which, at first, also astonished him, after having been so long used to the plain and highly practical advice which the rector, Mr. Larkyns, knew how to convey so well and so simply to his rustic hearers. But as soon as he had reflected on the very different characters of the two congregations, Mr. Verdant Green at once recognized the appropriateness of each class of sermons to its peculiar hearers; yet he could not altogether drive away the thought, how the generality of those who had on previous Sundays been his fellow-worshippers would open their blue Saxon eyes, and ransack their rustic brains, as to 'what *could* ha' come to rector,' if he were to indulge in Greek and Latin quotations, — *somewhat* after the following style. 'And though this interpretation may in these days be disputed, yet we shall find that it was once very generally received. For the learned St. Chrysostom is very clear on this point, where he says, 'Arma virumque cano, rusticus expectat, sub tegmine fagi'; of which the words of Irenaeus are a confirmation —{oto-totoio, papaperax, poluphloisboio thalassaes}.' Our hero, indeed, could not but help wondering what the fairer portion of the congregation made of these parts of the sermons, to whom, probably, the sentences just quoted would have sounded as full of meaning as those they really heard.

★ ★ ★

'Hallo, Gig-lamps!' said the cheery voice of little Mr. Bouncer, as he looked one morning into Verdant's rooms, followed by his two bull-terriers; 'why don't you sport something in the dog line? Something in the blood-hound or tarrier way. Ain't you fond o' dogs?'

'Oh, very!' replied our hero. 'I once had a very nice one, — a King Charles.'

'Oh!' observed Mr. Bouncer, 'one of them beggars that you have to feed with spring chickens, and get up with curling tongs. Ah! they're all very well in their way, and do for women and carriage-exercise; but give *me* this sort of thing!' and Mr. Bouncer patted one of his villainous looking pets, who wagged his corkscrew tail in reply. 'Now, these are beauties, and no mistake! What you call useful and ornamental; ain't you, Buzzy? The beggars are brothers; so I call them Huz and Buz:- Huz his first-born, you know, and Buz his brother.'

'I should like a dog,' said Verdant; 'but where could I keep one?'

'Oh, anywhere!' replied Mr. Bouncer confidently. 'I keep these beggars in the little shop for coal, just outside the door. It ain't the law, I know; but what's the odds as long as they're happy? *They* think it no end of a lark. I once had a Newfunland, and tried *him* there; but the obstinate brute considered it too small for him, and barked himself in such an unnatural manner, that at last he'd got no wool on the top of his head, — just the place where the wool ought to grow, you know; so I swopped the beggar to a Skimmery man for a regular slap-up set of pets of the ballet, framed and glazed, petticoats and all, mind you. But about your dog, Gig-lamps: -that cupboard there would be just the ticket; you could put him under the wine-bottles, and then there'd be wine above and whine below. *Videsne puer?* D'ye twig, young 'un? But if you're squeamish about that, there are heaps of places in the town where you could keep a beast.'

So, when our hero had been persuaded that the possession of an animal of the terrier species was absolutely necessary to a University man's existence, he had not to look about long without having the void filled up. Money will in most places procure any thing, from a grant of arms to a pair of wooden legs; so it is not surprising if, in Oxford, such an every-day commodity as a dog can be obtained through the medium of 'filthy lucre;' for there was a well-known dog-fancier and proprietor, whose surname was that of the rich substantive just mentioned, to which had been prefixed the 'filthy' adjective, probably for the sake of euphony. As usual, Filthy Lucre was clumping with his lame leg up and down the pavement just in front of the Brazenface gate, accompanied by his last 'new and extensive assortment' of terriers of every variety, which he now pulled up for the inspection of Mr. Verdant Green.

'Is it a long-aird dawg, or a smooth 'un, as you'd most fancy?' inquired Mr. Lucre. 'Har, sir!' he continued, in a flattering tone, as he saw our hero's eye dwelling on a Skye terrier; 'I see you're a gent as *does* know a good style of dawg, when you see 'un! It ain't often as you see a Skye sich as that, sir! Look at his colour, sir, and the way he looks out of his 'air! He answers to the name of *Mop*, sir, in consekvence of the length of his 'air; and he's cheap as dirt, sir, at four-ten! It's a throwin' of him away at the price; and I shouldn't do it, but I've got more dawgs than I've room for; so I'm obligated to make a sacrifice. Four-ten, sir! 'Ad the distemper, and everythink, and a reg'lar good 'un for the varmin.'

His merits also being testified to by Mr. Larkyns and Mr. Bouncer (who was considered a high authority in canine matters), and Verdant also liking the quaint appearance of the dog, *Mop* eventually became his property, for 'four-ten' *minus* five shillings, but *plus* a pint of buttery beer, which Mr. Lucre always pronounced to be customary 'in all dealins whatsumever atween gentlemen.' Verdant was highly gratified at possessing a real University dog, and he patted *Mop*, and said, 'Poo dog! poo Mop! poo fellow then!' and thought what a pet his sisters would make of him when he took him back home with him for the holi — the Vacation!

Mop was for following Mr. Lucre, who had clumped away up the street; and his new master had some difficulty in keeping him at his heels. By Mr. Bouncer's advice, he at once

138

took him over the river to the field opposite the Christ Church meadows, in order to test his rat-killing powers. How this could be done out in the open country, our hero was at a loss to know; but he discreetly held his tongue, for he was gradually becoming aware that a freshman in Oxford must live to learn, and that, as with most men, *experientia docet*.

They had just been punted over the river, and *Mop* had been restored to *terra firma*, when Mr. Bouncer's remark of 'There's the cove that'll do the trick for you!' directed Verdant's attention to an individual, who, from his general appearance, might have been first cousin to 'Filthy Lucre,' only that his live stock was of a different description. Slung from his shoulders was a large but shallow wire cage, in which were about a dozen doomed rats, whose futile endeavours to make their escape by running up the sides of their prison were regarded with the most intense earnestness by a group of terriers, who gave way to various phases of excitement. In his hand he carried a small circular cage, containing two or three rats for immediate use. On the receipt of sixpence, one of these was liberated; and a few yards start being (sportsmanlike) allowed, the speculator's terrier was then let loose, joined gratuitously, after a short interval, by a perfect pack in full cry, with a human chorus of 'Hoo rat! Too loo! loo dog!' The rat turned, twisted, doubled, became confused, was overtaken, and, with one grip and a shake, was dead; while the excited pack returned to watch and jump at the wire cages until another doomed prisoner was tossed forth to them. Gentlemen on their way for a walk were thus enabled to wile away a few minutes at the noble sport, and indulge themselves and their dogs with a little healthy excitement; while the boating costume of other gentlemen shewed that they had for a while left aquatic pursuits, and had strolled up from the river to indulge in 'the sports of the fancy.'

Although his new master invested several sixpences on *Mop's* behalf, yet that ungrateful animal, being of a passive temperament of mind as regarded rats, and a slow movement of body, in consequence of his long hair impeding his progress, rather disgraced himself by allowing the sport to be taken from his very teeth. But he still further disgraced himself, when he had been taken back to Brazenface, by howling all through the night in the cupboard where he had been placed, thereby setting on Mr. Bouncer's two bull-terriers, Huz and Buz, to echo the sounds with redoubled fury from their coal-hole quarters; thus causing loss of sleep and a great outlay of Saxon expletives to all the dwellers on the staircase. It was in vain that our hero got out of bed and opened the cupboard-door, and said, 'Poo Mop! good dog, then!' it was in vain that Mr. Bouncer shied boots at the coal-hole, and threatened Huz and Buz with loss of life; it was in vain that the tenant of the attic, Mr. Sloe, who was a reading-man, and sat up half the night, working for his degree, — it was in vain that he opened his door, and mildly declared (over the banisters), that it was impossible to get up Aristotle while such a noise was being made; it was in vain that Mr. Four-in-hand Fosbrooke, whose rooms were on the other side of Verdant's, came and administered to *Mop* severe punishment with a tandem-whip (it was a favourite boast with Mr. Fosbrooke, that he could flick a fly from his leader's ear); it was in vain to coax *Mop* with chicken-bones: he would neither be bribed nor frightened, and after a deceitful lull of a few minutes, just when every one was getting to sleep again, his melancholy howl would be raised with renewed vigour, and Huz and Buz would join for sympathy.

'I tell you what, Gig-lamps,' said Mr. Bouncer the next morning; 'this game'll never do. Bark's a very good thing to take in its proper way, when you're in want of it, and get it with port wine; but when you get it by itself and in too large doses, it ain't pleasant, you know. Huz and Buz are quiet enough, as long as they're let alone; and I should advise you to keep *Mop* down at Spavin's stables, or somewhere. But first, just let me give the brute the hiding he deserves.'

Poor *Mop* underwent his punishment like a martyr; and in the course of the day an arrangement was made with Mr. Spavin for *Mop's* board and lodging at his stables. But when Verdant called there the next day, for the purpose of taking him for a walk, there was no *Mop* to be found; taking advantage of the carelessness of one of Mr. Spavin's men, he had bolted through the open door, and made his escape. Mr. Bouncer, at a subsequent period, declared that he met *Mop* in the company of a well-known Regent-street fancier; but, however that may be, *Mop* was lost to Mr. Verdant Green.

10

Mr. Verdant Green Reforms his
Tailor's Bills and Runs Up Others. He also
Appears in a Rapid Act of Horsemanship,
and finds Isis Cool in Summer

The state of Mr. Verdant Green's outward
man had long offended Mr. Charles Larkyns'
more civilized taste; and he one day took
occasion delicately to hint to his friend, that it
would conduce more to his appearance as an
Oxford undergraduate, if he forswore the
primitive garments that his country-tailor had
condemned him to wear, and adapted the
'build' of his dress to the peculiar require-
ments of university fashion.

Acting upon this friendly hint, our
freshman at once betook himself to the shop
where he had bought his cap and gown, and
found its proprietor making use of the
invisible soap and washing his hands in the
imperceptible water, as though he had not left
that act of imaginary cleanliness since Verdant
and his father had last seen him.

'Oh, certainly, sir; an abundant variety,' was
his reply to Verdant's question, if he could

show him any patterns that were fashionable in Oxford. 'The greatest stock hout of London, I should say, sir, decidedly. This is a nice unpretending gentlemanly thing, sir, that we make up a good deal!' and he spread a shaggy substance before the freshman's eyes.

'What do you make it up for?' inquired our hero, who thought it more nearly resembled the hide of his lamented *Mop* than any other substance.

'Oh, morning garments, sir! Reading and walking-coats, for erudition and the promenade, sir! Looks well with vest of the same material, sprinkled down with coral currant buttons! We've some sweet things in vests, sir; and some neat, quiet trouserings, that I'm sure would give satisfaction.' And the tailor and robe-maker, between washings with the invisible soap, so visibly 'soaped' our hero in what is understood to be the shop-sense of the word, and so surrounded him with a perfect irradiation of aggressive patterns of oriental gorgeousness, that Mr. Verdant Green became bewildered, and finally made choice of one of the unpretending gentlemanly *Mop*-like coats, and 'vest and trouserings,' of a neat, quiet, plaid-pattern, in red and green, which, he was informed, were all the rage.

When these had been sent home to him,

together with a neck-tie of Oxford-blue from Randall's, and an immaculate guinea Lincoln-and-Bennett, our hero was delighted with the general effect of the costume; and after calling in at the tailor's to express his approbation, he at once sallied forth to 'do the High,' and display his new purchases. A drawn silk bonnet of pale lavender, from which floated some bewitching ringlets, quickly attracted our hero's attention; and the sight of an arch, French-looking face, which (to his short-sighted imagination) smiled upon him as the young lady rustled by, immediately plunged him into the depths of first-love. Without the slightest encouragement being given him, he stalked this little deer to her lair, and, after some difficulty, discovered the enchantress to be Mademoiselle Mouslin de Laine, one of the presiding goddesses of a fancy hosiery warehouse. There, for the next fortnight, — until which immense period his ardent passion had not subsided, — our hero was daily to be seen purchasing articles for which he had no earthly use, but fully recompensed for his outlay by the artless (ill-natured people said, artful) smiles, and engaging, piquant conversation of mademoiselle. Our hero, when reminded of this at a subsequent period, protested that he had thus acted merely to improve his French, and only conversed with mademoiselle for educational purposes. But we have our doubts. *Credat Judaeus!*

About this time also our hero laid the nest-eggs for a very promising brood of bills, by acquiring an expensive habit of strolling in to shops, and purchasing 'an extensive assortment of articles of every description,' for no other consideration than that he should not be called upon to pay for them until he had taken his degree. He also decorated the walls of his rooms with choice specimens of engravings: for the turning over of portfolios at Ryman's, and Wyatt's, usually leads to the eventual turning over of a considerable amount of cash; and our hero had not yet become acquainted with the cheaper circulating-system of pictures, which gives you a fresh set every term, and passes on your old ones to some other subscriber. But, in the meantime, it is very delightful, when you admire any thing, to be able to say, 'Send that to my room!' and to be obsequiously obeyed, 'no questions asked,' and no payment demanded; and as for the future, why — as Mr. Larkyns observed, as they strolled down the High — 'I suppose the bills *will* come in some day or other, but the governor will see to them; and though he may grumble and pull a long face, yet he'll only be too glad you've got your degree, and, in the fulness of his heart, he will open his cheque-book. I daresay old Horace gives very good advice when he says, 'carpe diem'; but when he adds, 'quam minimum credula postero,' [14] about 'not giving the least credit to the succeeding day,' it is clear that he never looked forward to the Oxford tradesmen and the credit-system. Do you ever read Wordsworth, Verdant?' continued Mr. Larkyns, as they stopped at the corner of Oriel Street, to look in at a spacious range of shop-windows, that were crowded with a costly and glittering profusion of *papier mache* articles, statuettes, bronzes, glass, and every kind of 'fancy goods' that could be classed as 'art-workmanship.'

'Why, I've not read much of Wordsworth myself,' replied our hero; 'but I've heard my sister Mary read a great deal of his poetry.'

'Shews her taste,' said Charles Larkyns. 'Well, this shop — you see the name — is Spiers'; and Wordsworth, in his sonnet to Oxford, has immortalized him. Don't you remember the lines?-

'O ye Spiers of Oxford! your presence overpowers
The soberness of reason!'

It was very queer that Wordsworth should ascribe to Messrs. Spiers all the intoxication of the place; but then he was a Cambridge man, and prejudiced. Nice shop, though, isn't it? Particularly useful, and no less ornamental. It's one of the greatest lounges of the place. Let us go in and have a look at what Mrs. Caudle calls the articles of bigotry and virtue.'

Mr. Verdant Green was soon deeply engaged in an inspection of those *papier-mache* 'remembrances of Oxford' for which the Messrs. Spiers are so justly famed; but after turning over tables, trays, screens, desks, albums, portfolios, and other things, — all of which displayed views of Oxford from every variety of aspect, and were executed with such truth and perception of the higher qualities of art, that they formed in themselves quite a small but gratuitous Academy exhibition, — our hero became so confused among the bewildering allurements around him, as to feel quite an *embarras de richesses*, and to be in a state of mind in which he was nearly giving Mr. Spiers the most extensive (and expensive) order which probably that gentleman had ever received from an undergraduate. Fortunately for his purse, his attention was somewhat distracted by perceiving that Mr. Slowcoach was at his elbow, looking over ink-stands and reading-lamps, and also by Charles Larkyns calling upon him to decide whether he should have the cigar-case he had purchased emblazoned with the heraldic device of the Larkyns, or illuminated with the Euripidean motto,-

To bakchikon doraema labe, se gar philo.

When this point had been decided, Mr. Larkyns proposed to Verdant that he should astonish and delight his governor by having the Green arms emblazoned on a fire-screen, and taking it home with him as a gift. 'Or else,' he said, 'order one with the garden-view of Brazenface, and then they'll have more satisfaction in looking at that than at one of those offensive cockatoos, in an arabesque landscape, under a bronze sky, which usually sprawls over every thing that is *papier mache*. But you won't see that sort of thing here; so you can't well go wrong, whatever you buy.' Finally, Mr. Verdant Green (N.B. Mr. Green, senior, would have eventually to pay the bill) ordered a fire-screen to be prepared with the family-arms, as a present for his father; a ditto, with the view of his college, for his mother; a writing-case, with the High Street view, for his aunt; a netting-box, card-case, and a model of the Martyrs' Memorial, for his three sisters; and having thus bountifully remembered his family-circle, he treated himself with a modest paper-knife, and was treated in return by Mr. Spiers with a perfect *bijou* of art, in the shape of 'a memorial for visitors to Oxford,' in which the chief glories of that city were set forth in gold and colours, in the most attractive form, and which our hero immediately posted off to the Manor Green.

'And now, Verdant,' said Mr. Larkyns, 'you may just as well get a hack, and come for a ride with me. You've kept up your riding, of course.'

'Oh, yes — a little!' faltered our hero.

Now, the reader may perhaps remember, that in an early part of our veracious chronicle we hinted that Mr. Verdant Green's equestrian performances were but of a humble character. They were, in fact, limited to an occasional ride with his sisters when they required a cavalier; but on these occasions, the old cob, which Verdant called his own, was warranted not to kick, or plunge, or start, or do anything derogatory to its age and infirmities. So that Charles Larkyns' proposition caused him some little nervous agitation; nevertheless, as he was ashamed to confess his fears, he, in a moment of weakness, consented to accompany his friend.

'We'll go to Symonds',' said Mr. Larkyns; 'I keep my hack there; and you can depend upon having a good one.'

So they made their way to Holywell Street, and turned under a gateway, and up a paved yard, to the stables. The upper part of the yard was littered down with straw, and covered in by a light, open roof; and in the stables there was accommodation for a hundred horses. At the back of the stables, and separated from the Wadham Gardens by a narrow lane, was a paddock; and here they found Mr. Fosbrooke, and one or two of his friends, inspecting the leaping abilities of a fine hunter, which one of the stable-boys was taking backwards and forwards over the hurdles and fences erected for that purpose.

The horses were soon ready, and Verdant summoned up enough courage to say, with the Count in *Mazeppa*, 'Bring forth the steed!' And when the steed was brought, in all the exuberance of (literally) animal spirits, he felt that he was about to be another Mazeppa, and perform feats on the back of a wild horse; and he could not help saying to the ostler, 'He looks rather-vicious, I'm afraid!'

'Wicious, sir,' replied the groom; 'bless you, sir! she's as sweet-tempered as any young ooman you ever paid your intentions to. The mare's as quiet a mare as was ever crossed;

this 'ere's ony her play at comin' fresh out of the stable!'

Verdant, however, had a presentiment that the play would soon become earnest; but he seated himself in the saddle (after a short delirious dance on one toe), and in a state of extreme agitation, not to say perspiration, proceeded at a walk, by Mr. Larkyns' side, up Holywell Street. Here the mare, who doubtless soon understood what sort of rider she had got on her back, began to be more demonstrative of the 'fresh'ness of her animal spirits. Broad Street was scarcely broad enough to contain the series of *tableaux vivants* and heraldic attitudes that she assumed. 'Don't pull the curb-rein so!' shouted Charles Larkyns; but Verdant was in far too dreadful a state of mind to understand what he said, or even to know which *was* the curb-rein; and after convulsively clutching at the mane and the pommel, in his endeavours to keep his seat, he first 'lost his head,' and then his seat, and ignominiously gliding over the mare's tail, found that his lodging was on the cold ground. Relieved of her burden, the mare quietly trotted back to her stables; while Verdant, finding himself unhurt, got up, replaced his hat and spectacles, and registered a mental vow never to mount an Oxford hack again.

'Never mind, old fellow!' said Charles Larkyns, consolingly; 'these little accidents *will* occur, you know, even with the best regulated riders! There were not *more* than a dozen ladies saw you, though you certainly made very creditable exertions to ride over one or two of them. Well! if you say you won't go back to Symonds', and get another hack, I must go on solus; but I shall see you at the Bump-supper to-night! I got old Blades to ask you to it. I'm going now in search of an appetite, and I should advise you to take a turn round the Parks and do the same. *Au reservoir!*'

So our hero, after he had compensated the livery-stable keeper, followed his friend's advice, and strolled round the neatly-kept potato-gardens denominated 'the Parks,' looking in vain for the deer that have never been there, and finding them represented only by nursery-maids and — others.

★ ★ ★

Mr. Blades, familiarly known as 'old Blades' and 'Billy,' was a gentleman who was fashioned somewhat after the model of the torso of Hercules; and, as Stroke of the Brazenface boat, was held in high estimation, not only by the men of his own college, but also by the boating men of the University at large. His University existence seemed to be engaged in one long struggle, the end and aim of which was to place the Brazenface boat in that envied position known in aquatic anatomy as 'the head of the river;' and in this struggle all Mr. Blades' energies of mind and body, — though particularly of body, — were engaged. Not a freshman was allowed to enter Brazenface, but immediately Mr. Blades' eye was upon him; and if the expansion of the upper part of his coat and waistcoat denoted that his muscular development of chest and arms was of a kind that might be serviceable to the great object aforesaid — the placing of the Brazenface boat at the head of the river, — then Mr. Blades came and made flattering proposals to the new-comer to assist in the great work. But he was also indefatigable, as secretary to his college club, in seeking out all freshmen, even if their thews and sinews were not muscular models, and inducing them to aid the glorious cause by becoming members of the club.

A Bump-supper — that is, O ye uniniti-ated! a supper to commemorate the fact of the boat of one college having, in the annual races, bumped, or touched the boat of another college immediately in its front, thereby gaining a place towards the head of the river, — a Bump-supper was a famous opportunity for discovering both the rowing and paying capabilities of freshmen, who, in the enthusiasm of the moment, would put down their two or three guineas, and at once propose their names to be enrolled as members at the next meeting of the club.

And thus it was with Mr. Verdant Green, who, before the evening was over, found that he had not only given in his name ('proposed by Charles Larkyns, Esq., seconded by Henry Bouncer, Esq.'), but that a desire was burning within his breast to distinguish himself in aquatic pursuits. Scarcely any thing else was talked of during the whole evening but the prospective chances of Brazenface bumping Balliol and Brasenose, and thereby getting to the head of the river. It was also mysteriously whispered, that Worcester and Christ Church were doing well, and might prove formidable; and that Exeter, Lincoln, and Wadham were very shady, and not doing the things that were expected of them. Great excitement too was caused by the announcement, that the Balliol stroke had knocked up, or knocked down, or done some thing which Mr. Verdant Green concluded he ought not to have done; and that the Brasenose bow had been seen with a cigar in his mouth, and also eating pastry in Hall, — things shocking in themselves, and quite contrary to all training principles. Then there were anticipations of Henley; and criticisms on the new eight out-rigger that Searle was laying down for the University crew; and comparisons between somebody's stroke and somebody else's spurt; and a good deal of reference to Clasper and Coombes, and Newall and Pococke, who might have been heathen deities for all that our hero knew, and from the manner in which they were mentioned.

The aquatic desires that were now burning in Mr. Verdant Green's breast could only be put out by the water; so to the river he next day went, and, by Charles Larkyns' advice, made his first essay in a 'tub' from Hall's. Being a complete novice with the oars, our hero had no sooner pulled off his coat and given a pull, than he succeeded in catching a tremendous 'crab,' the effect of which was to throw him backwards, and almost to upset the boat. Fortunately, however, 'tubs' recover their equilibrium almost as easily as tombolas, and 'the Sylph' did not belie its character; so the freshman again assumed a proper position, and was shoved off with a boat-hook. At first he made some hopeless splashes in the stream, the only effect of which was to make the boat turn with a circular movement towards Folly Bridge; but Charles Larkyns at once came to the rescue with the simple but energetic compendium of boating instruction, 'Put your oar in deep, and bring it out with a jerk!'

Bearing this in mind, our hero's efforts met with well-merited success; and he soon passed that mansion which, instead of cellars, appears to have an ingenious system of small rivers to thoroughly irrigate its foundations. One by one, too, he passed those house-boats which are more like the Noah's arks of toy-shops than anything else, and sometimes contain quite as original a mixture of animal specimens. Warming with his exertions, Mr. Verdant Green passed the University barge in great style, just as the eight was preparing to start; and though he was not able to 'feather his oars with skill and dexterity,' like the jolly young waterman in the song, yet his sleight-of-hand performances with them proved not only a source of great satisfaction to the crews on the river, but also to the promenaders on the shore.

He had left the Christ Church meadows far behind, and was beginning to feel slightly exhausted by his unwonted exertions, when he reached that bewildering part of the river termed 'the Gut.' So confusing were the intestine commotions of this gut, that, after passing a chequered existence as an aquatic shuttlecock, and being assailed with a slang-dictionary-full of opprobrious epithets, Mr. Verdant Green caught another tremendous crab, and before he could recover himself, the 'tub' received a shock, and, with a loud cry of 'Boat ahead!' ringing in his ears, the University Eight passed over the place where he and 'the Sylph' had so lately disported themselves.

With the wind nearly knocked out of his body by the blade of the bow-oar striking him on the chest as he rose to the surface, our unfortunate hero was immediately dragged from the water, in a condition like that of the child in *The Stranger* (the only joke, by the way, in that most dreary play) 'not dead, but very wet!' and forthwith placed in safety in his deliverer's boat.

'Hallo, Gig-lamps! who the doose had thought of seeing you here, devouring Isis in this expensive way!' said a voice very coolly. And our hero found that he had been rescued by little Mr. Bouncer, who had been tacking up the river in company with Huz and Buz and his meerschaum. 'You *have* been and gone and done it now, young man!' continued the vivacious little gentleman, as he surveyed our hero's draggled and forlorn condition. 'If you'd only a comb and a glass in your hand, you'd look distressingly like a cross-breed with a mermaid! You ain't subject to the whatdyecallems — the rheumatics, are you? Because, if so, I could put you on shore at a tidy little shop where you can get a glass of brandy-and-water, and have your clothes dried; and then mamma won't scold.'

'Indeed,' chattered our hero, 'I shall be very glad indeed; for I feel — rather cold. But what am I to do with my boat?'

'Oh, the Lively Polly, or whatever her name is, will find her way back safe enough. There are plenty of boatmen on the river who'll see to her and take her back to her owner; and if you got her from Hall's, I daresay she'll dream that she's dreamt in marble halls, like you did, Gig-lamps, that night at Smalls', when you got wet in rather a more lively style than you've done to-day. Now I'll tack you up to that little shop I told you of.'

So there our hero was put on shore, and Mr. Bouncer made fast his boat and accompanied him; and did not leave him until he had seen him between the blankets, drinking a glass of hot brandy-and-water, the while his clothes were smoking before the fire.

This little adventure (for a time at least) checked Mr. Verdant Green's aspirations to distinguish himself on the river; and he therefore renounced the sweets of the Isis, and contented himself by practising with a punt on the Cherwell. There, after repeatedly overbalancing himself in the most suicidal manner, he at length peacefully settled down into the lounging blissfulness of a 'Cherwell water-lily;' and on the hot days, among those gentlemen who had moored their punts underneath the overhanging boughs of the willows and limes, and beneath their cool shade were lying, in *dolce far niente* fashion, with their legs up and a weed in their mouth, reading the last new novel, or some less immaculate work, — among these gentlemen might haply have been discerned the form and spectacles of Mr. Verdant Green.

11

Mr. Verdant Green's
Sports and Pastimes

Archery was all the fashion at Brazenface. They had as fine a lawn for it as the Trinity men had; and all day long there was somebody to be seen making holes in the targets, and endeavouring to realize the *pose* of the Apollo Belvidere; — rather a difficult thing to do, when you come to wear plaid trousers and shaggy coats. As Mr. Verdant Green felt desirous not only to uphold all the institutions of the University, but also to make himself acquainted with the sports and pastimes of the place, he forthwith joined the Archery and Cricket Clubs. He at once inspected the manufactures of Muir and Buchanan; and after selecting from their stores a fancy-wood bow, with arrows, belt, quiver, guard, tips, tassels, and grease-pot, he felt himself to be duly prepared to represent the Toxophilite character. But the sustaining it was a more difficult thing than he had conceived; for although he thought that it would be next to impossible to miss a shot when the target was so large, and the arrow went so easily from the bow, yet our hero soon discovered that even in the first steps of archery there was something to be learnt, and that the mere stringing of his bow was a performance attended with considerable difficulty. It was always slipping from his instep, or twisting the wrong way, or threatening to snap in sunder, or refusing to allow his fingers to slip the knot, or doing something that was dreadfully uncomfortable, and productive of perspiration; and two or three times he was reduced to the abject necessity of asking his friends to string his bow for him.

But when he had mastered this slight difficulty, he found that the arrows (to use Mr. Bouncer's phrase) 'wobbled,' and had a predilection for going anywhere but into the target, notwithstanding its size; and unfortunately one went into the body of the Honourable Mr. Stormer's favourite Skye terrier, though, thanks to its shaggy coat and the bluntness of the arrow, it did not do a great amount of mischief; nevertheless, the vials of Mr. Stormer's wrath were outpoured upon Mr. Verdant Green's head; and such *epea pteroenta* followed the winged arrow, that our hero became alarmed, and for the time forswore archery practice.

As he had fully equipped himself for archery, so also Mr. Verdant Green, (on the authority of Mr. Bouncer) got himself up for cricket regardless of expense; and he made his first appearance in the field in a straw hat with blue ribbon, and 'flannels,' and spiked shoes of perfect propriety. As Mr. Bouncer had told him that, in cricket, attitude was every thing, Verdant, as soon as he went in for his innings, took up what he considered to be a very good position at the wicket. Little Mr. Bouncer, who was bowling, delivered the ball with a swiftness that seemed rather astonishing in such a small gentleman. The first ball was 'wide;' nevertheless, Verdant (after it had passed) struck at it, raising his bat high in the air, and bringing it straight down to the ground as though it were an executioner's axe. The second ball was nearer to the mark; but it came in with such swiftness, that, as Mr. Verdant Green was quite new to round bowling, it was rather too quick for him, and hit him severely on the — , well, never mind, — on the trousers.

'Hallo, Gig-lamps!' shouted the delighted Mr. Bouncer, 'nothing like backing up; but it's no use assuming a stern appearance; you'll get your hand in soon, old feller!'

But Verdant found that before he could get his hand in, the ball was got into his wicket;

and that while he was preparing for the strike, the ball shot by; and, as Mr. Stumps, the wicket-keeper, kindly informed him, 'there was a row in his timber-yard.' Thus Verdant's score was always on the *lucus a non lucendo* principle of derivation, for not even to a quarter of a score did it ever reach; and he felt that he should never rival a Mynn or be a Parr with any one of the 'All England' players.

Besides these out-of-door sports, our hero also devoted a good deal of his time to acquiring in-door games, being quickly initiated into the mysteries of billiards, and plunging headlong into pool. It was in the billiard-room that Verdant first formed his acquaintance with Mr. Fluke of Christ Church, well known to be the best player in the University, and who, if report spoke truly, always made his five hundred a year by his skill in the game. Mr. Fluke kindly put our hero 'into the way to become a player;' and Verdant soon found the apprenticeship was attended with rather heavy fees.

At the wine-parties also that he attended he became rather a greater adept at cards than he had formerly been. 'Van John' was the favourite game; and he was not long in discovering that taking shillings and half-crowns, instead of counters and 'fish,' and going odds on the colours, and losing five pounds before he was aware of it, was a very different thing to playing *vingt-et-un* at home with his sisters for 'love' — (though perhaps cards afford the only way in which young ladies at twenty-one will *play* for love).

In returning to Brazenface late from these parties, our hero was sometimes frightfully alarmed by suddenly finding himself face to face with a dreadful apparition, to which, by constant familiarity, he gradually became accustomed, and learned to look upon as the proctor with his marshal and bulldogs. At first, too, he was on such occasions greatly alarmed at finding the gates of Brazenface closed, obliging him thereby to 'knock-in;' and not only did he apologize to the porter for troubling him to open the wicket, but he also volunteered elaborate explanations of the reasons that had kept him out after time, — explanations that were not received in the spirit with which they were tendered. When our freshman became aware of the mysteries of a gate-bill, he felt more at his ease.

Mr. Verdant Green learned many things during his freshman's term, and, among others, he discovered that the quiet retirement of college-rooms, of which he had heard so much, was in many cases an unsubstantial idea, founded on imagination, and built up by fancy. One day that he had been writing a letter in Mr. Smalls' rooms, which were on the ground-floor, Verdant congratulated himself that his own rooms were on the third floor, and were thus removed from the possibility of his friends, when he had sported his oak, being able to get through his window to 'chaff' him; but he soon discovered that rooms upstairs had also objectionable points in their private character, and were not altogether such eligible apartments as he had at first anticipated. First, there was the getting up and down the dislocated staircase, a feat which at night was sometimes attended with difficulty. Then, when he had accomplished this feat, there was no way of escaping from the noise of his neighbours. Mr. Sloe, the reading-man in the garret above, was one of those abominable nuisances, a peripatetic student, who 'got up' every subject by pacing up and down his limited apartment, and, like the sentry, 'walked his dreary round' at unseasonable hours of the night, at which time could be plainly heard the wretched chuckle, and crackings of knuckles (Mr. Sloe's way of expressing intense delight), with which he welcomed some miserable joke of Aristophanes, painfully elaborated by the help of Liddell-and-Scott; or the disgustingly sonorous way in which he declaimed his

Greek choruses. This was bad enough at night; but in the day-time there was a still greater nuisance. The rooms immediately beneath Verdant's were possessed by a gentleman whose musical powers were of an unusually limited description, but who, unfortunately for his neighbours, possessed the idea that the cornet-a-piston was a beautiful instrument for pic-nics, races, boating-parties, and other long-vacation amusements, and sedulously practised 'In my cottage near a wood,' 'Away with melancholy,' and other airs of a lively character, in a doleful and distracted way, that would have fully justified his immediate homicide, or, at any rate, the confiscation of his offending instrument.

Then, on the one side of Verdant's room, was Mr. Bouncer, sounding his octaves, and 'going the complete unicorn;' and his bull-terriers, Huz and Buz, all and each of whom were of a restless and loud temperament; while, on the other side, were Mr. Four-in-hand Fosbrooke's rooms, in which fencing, boxing, single-stick, and other violent sports, were gone through, with a great expenditure of 'Sa-ha! sa-ha!' and stampings. Verdant was sometimes induced to go in, and never could sufficiently admire the way in which men could be rapped with single-sticks without crying out or flinching;

for it made him almost sore even to look at them. Mr. Blades, the stroke, was a frequent visitor there, and developed his muscles in the most satisfactory manner.

After many refusals, our hero was at length persuaded to put on the gloves, and have a friendly bout with Mr. Blades. The result was as might have been anticipated; and Mr. Smalls doubtless gave a very correct *resume* of the proceeding (for, as we have before said, he was thoroughly conversant with the sporting slang of *Tintinnabulum's Life*), when he told Verdant, that his claret had been repeatedly tapped, his bread-basket walked into, his daylights darkened, his ivories rattled, his nozzle barked, his whisker-bed napped heavily, his kissing-trap countered, his ribs roasted, his nut spanked, and his whole person put in chancery, stung, bruised, fibbed, propped, fiddled, slogged, and otherwise ill-treated. So it is hardly to be wondered at if Mr. Verdant Green from thenceforth gave up boxing, as a senseless and ungentlemanly amusement.

But while these pleasures(?) of the body were being attended to, the recreation of the mind was not forgotten. Mr. Larkyns had proposed Verdant's name at the Union; and, to that gentleman's great satisfaction, he was not black-balled. He daily, therefore, frequented the reading-room, and made a point

168

of looking through all the magazines and newspapers; while he felt quite a pride in sitting in luxurious state upstairs, writing his letters to the home department on the very best note-paper, and sealing them extensively with 'the Oxford Union' seal; though he could not at first be persuaded that trusting his letters to a wire closet was at all a safe system of postage.

He also attended the Debates, which were then held in the long room behind Wyatt's; and he was particularly charmed with the manner in which vital questions, that (as he learned from the newspapers) had proved stumbling-blocks to the greatest statesmen of the land, were rapidly solved by the embryo statesmen of the Oxford Union. It was quite a sight, in that long picture-room, to see the rows of light iron seats densely crowded with young men — some of whom would perhaps rise to be Cannings, or Peels, or Gladstones — and to hear how one beardless gentleman would call another beardless gentleman his 'honourable friend,' and appeal 'to the sense of the House,' and address himself to 'Mr. Speaker;' and how they would all juggle the same tricks of rhetoric as their fathers were doing in certain other debates in a certain other House. And it was curious, too, to mark the points of resemblance between the two

Houses; and how the smaller one had, on its smaller scale, its Hume, and its Lord John, and its 'Dizzy;' and how they went through the same traditional forms, and preserved the same time-honoured ideas, and debated in the fullest houses, with the greatest spirit and the greatest length, on such points as, 'What course is it advisable for this country to take in regard to the government of its Indian possessions, and the imprisonment of Mr. Jones by the Rajah of Humbugpoopoonah?'

Indeed, Mr. Verdant Green was so excited by this interesting debate, that on the third night of its adjournment he rose to address the House; but being 'no orator as Brutus is,' his few broken words were received with laughter, and the honourable gentleman was coughed down.

Our hero had, as an Oxford freshman, to go through that cheerful form called 'sitting in the schools,' — a form which consisted in the following ceremony. Through a door in the right-hand corner of the Schools Quadrangle, — (Oh, that door! does it not bring a pang into your heart only to think of it? to remember the day when you went in there as pale as the little pair of bands in which you were dressed for your sacrifice; and came out all in a glow and a chill when your examination was over; and posted your bosom-friend there to receive from Purdue the little slip of paper, and bring you the thrilling intelligence that you had passed; or to come empty-handed, and say that you had been plucked!

Oh that door! well might be inscribed there the line which, on Dante's authority, is assigned to the door of another place, —

'ALL HOPE ABANDON, YE WHO ENTER HERE!'

— entering through this door in company with several other unfortunates, our hero passed between two galleries through a passage, by which, if the place had been a circus, the horses would have entered, and found himself in a tolerably large room lighted on either side by windows, and panelled half-way up the walls. Down the centre of this room ran a large green-baize-covered table, on the one side of which were some eight or ten miserable beings who were then undergoing examination, and were supplied with pens, ink, blotting-pad, and large sheets of thin 'scribble-paper,' on which they were struggling to impress their ideas; or else had a book set before them, out of which they were construing, or being racked with questions that touched now on one subject and now on another, like a bee among flowers. The large table was liberally supplied with all the apparatus and instruments of torture; and on the other side of it sat the three examiners, as dreadful and formidable as the terrible three of Venice.

At the upper end of the room was a chair of state for the Vice-Chancellor, whenever he deigned to personally superintend the torture; to the right and left of which accommodation was provided for other victims. On the right hand of the room was a small open gallery of two seats (like those seen in infant schools); and here, from 10 in the morning till 4 in the afternoon, with only the interval of a quarter of an hour for luncheon, Mr. Verdant Green was compelled to sit and watch the proceedings, his perseverance being attested to by a certificate which he received as a reward for his meritorious conduct. If this 'sitting in the schools' was established as an *in terrorem* form for the spectators, it undoubtedly generally had the desired effect; and what with the misery of sitting through a whole day on a hard bench with nothing to do, and the agony of seeing your fellow-creatures plucked, and having visions of the same prospective fate for yourself, the day on which the sitting takes place was usually regarded as one of those which, 'if 'twere done, 'twere well it should be done quickly.'

As an appropriate sequel to this proceeding, Mr. Verdant Green attended the interesting ceremony of conferring degrees; where he discovered that the apparently insane promenade of the proctor gave rise to the name bestowed on (what Mr. Larkyns called) the equally insane custom of 'plucking.' There too our hero saw the Vice-Chancellor in all his glory; and so agreeable were the proceedings, that altogether he had a great deal of Bliss.

12

Mr. Verdant Green Terminates
his Existence as an Oxford Freshman

'Before I go home,' said Mr. Verdant Green, as he expelled a volume of smoke from his lips, — for he had overcome his first weakness, and now 'took his weed' regularly, — 'before I go home, I must see what I owe in the place; for my father said he did not like for me to run in debt, but wished me to settle my bills terminally.'

'What, you're afraid of having what we call bill-ious fever, I suppose, eh?' laughed Charles Larkyns. 'All exploded ideas, my dear fellow. They do very well in their way, but they don't answer; don't pay, in fact; and the shopkeepers don't like it either. By the way, I can shew you a great curiosity; — the autograph of an Oxford tradesman, *very rare*! I think of presenting it to the Ashmolean.' And Mr. Larkyns opened his writing-desk, and took therefrom an Oxford pastrycook's bill, on which appeared the magic word, 'Received.'

'Now, there is one thing,' continued Mr.

Larkyns, 'which you really must do before you go down, and that is to see Blenheim. And the best thing that you can do is to join Fosbrooke and Bouncer and me, in a trap to Woodstock to-morrow. We'll go in good time, and make a day of it.'

Verdant readily agreed to make one of the party; and the next morning, after a breakfast in Charles Larkyns' rooms, they made their way to a side street leading out of Beaumont Street, where the dog-cart was in waiting. As it was drawn by two horses, placed in tandem fashion, Mr. Fosbrooke had an opportunity of displaying his Jehu powers; which he did to great advantage, not allowing his leader to run his nose into the cart, and being enabled to turn sharp corners without chipping the bricks, or running the wheel up the bank.

They reached Woodstock after a very pleasant ride, and clattered up its one long street to the principal hotel; but Mr. Fosbrooke whipped into the yard to the left so rapidly, that our hero, who was not much used to the back seat of a dog-cart, flew off by some means at a tangent to the right, and was consequently degraded in the eyes of the inhabitants.

After ordering for dinner every thing that the house was enabled to supply, they made their way in the first place (as it could only be seen between 11 and 1) to Blenheim; the princely splendours of which were not only costly in themselves, but, as our hero soon found, costly also to the sight-seer. The doors in the *suite* of apartments were all opposite to each other, so that, as a crimson cord was passed from one to the other, the spectator was kept entirely to the one side of the room, and merely a glance could be obtained of the Raffaelle, the glorious Rubenses, the Vandycks, and the almost equally fine Sir Joshuas. But even the glance they had was but a passing one, as the servant trotted them through the rooms with the rapidity of locomotion and explanation of a Westminster Abbey verger; and he made a fierce attack on Verdant, who had lagged behind, and was short-sightedly peering at the celebrated 'Charles the First' of Vandyck, as though he had lingered in order to surreptitiously appropriate some of the tables, couches, and other trifling articles that ornamented the rooms. In this way they went at railroad pace through the *suite* of rooms and the library, — where the chief thing pointed out appeared to be a grease-mark on the floor made by somebody at somebody else's wedding-breakfast, — and to the chapel, where they admired the ingenuity of the sparrows and other birds that built about

Rysbrach's monumental mountain of marble to the memory of the Duke and Duchess of Marlborough; — and then to the so-called 'Titian room' (shade of mighty Titian, forgive the insult!) where they saw the Loves of the Gods represented in the most unloveable manner, and where a flunkey lounged lazily at the door, and, in spite of Mr. Bouncer's expostulatory 'chaff,' demanded half-a-crown for the sight.

Indeed, the sight-seeing at Blenheim seemed to be a system of half-crowns. The first servant would take them a little way, and then say, 'I don't go any further, sir; half-a-crown!' and hand them over to servant number two, who, after a short interval, would pass them on (half-a-crown!) to the servant who shewed the chapel (half-a-crown!), who would forward them on to the 'Titian' Gallery (half-a-crown!), who would hand them over to the flower-garden (half-a-crown!), who would entrust them to the rose-garden (half-a-crown!), who would give them up to another, who shewed parts of the Park, and the rest of it. Somewhat in this manner an Oxford party sees Blenheim (the present of the nation); and Mr. Verdant Green found it the most expensive show-place he had ever seen.

Some of the Park, however, was free

(though they were two or three times ordered to 'get off the grass'); and they rambled about among the noble trees, and admired the fine views of the Hall, and smoked their weeds, and became very pathetic at Rosamond's Spring. They then came back into Woodstock, which they found to be like all Oxford towns, only rather duller perhaps, the principal signs of life being some fowls lazily pecking about in the grass-grown street, and two cats sporting without fear of interruption from a dog, who was too much overcome by the *ennui* of the place to interfere with them.

Mr. Bouncer then led the way to an inn, where the bar was presided over by a young lady, 'on whom,' he said, 'he was desperately sweet,' and with whom he conversed in the most affable and brotherly manner, and for whom also he had brought, as an appropriate present, a Book of Comic Songs; 'for,' said the little gentleman, 'hang it! she's a girl of what you call *mind*, you know! and she's heard of the opera, and begun the piano, — though she don't get much time, you see, for it in the bar, — and she sings regular slap-up, and no mistake!'

So they left this young lady drawing bitter beer for Mr. Bouncer, and otherwise attending to her adorer's wants, and endeavoured to have a game of billiards on a wooden table that had no cushions, with curious cues that had no leathers. Slightly failing in this difficult game, they strolled about till dinner-time, when Mr. Verdant Green became mysteriously lost for some time, and was eventually found by Charles Larkyns and Mr. Fosbrooke in a glover's shop, where he was sitting on a high stool, and basking in the sunshiny smiles of two 'neat little glovers.' Our hero at first feigned to be simply making purchases of Woodstock gloves and purses, as *souvenirs* of his visit, and presents for his sisters; but in the course of the evening, being greatly 'chaffed' on the subject, he began to exercise his imagination, and talk of the 'great fun' he had had; — though what particular fun there may be in smiling amiably across a counter at a feminine shopkeeper who is selling you gloves, it is hard to say: perhaps Dr. Sterne could help us to an answer.

They spent altogether a very lively day; and after a rather protracted sitting over their wine, they returned to Oxford with great hilarity, Mr. Bouncer's post-horn coming out with great effect in the stillness of the moonlight night. Unfortunately their mirth was somewhat checked when they had got as far as Peyman's Gate; for the proctor, with mistaken kindness, had taken the trouble to meet them there, lest they should escape him by entering Oxford by any devious way; and the marshal and the bull-dogs were at the leader's head just as Mr. Fosbrooke was triumphantly guiding them through the turnpike. Verdant gave up his name and that of his college with a thrill of terror, and nearly fell off the drag from fright, when he was told to call upon the proctor the next morning.

'Keep your pecker up, old feller!' said Mr. Bouncer, in an encouraging tone, as they drove into Oxford, 'and don't be down in the mouth about a dirty trick like this. He won't hurt you much, Gig-lamps! Gate and chapel you; or give you some old Greek party to write out; or send you down to your mammy for a twelve-month; or some little trifle of that sort. I only wish the beggar would come up our staircase! if Huz, and Buz his brother, didn't do their duty by him, it would be doosid odd. Now, don't you go and get bad dreams, Gig-lamps! because it don't pay; and you'll soon get used to these sort of things; and what's the odds, as long as you're happy? I like to take things coolly, I do.'

To judge from Mr. Bouncer's serenity, and the far-from-nervous manner in which he 'sounded his octaves,' *he* at least appeared to be thoroughly used to 'that sort of thing,' and doubtless slept as tranquilly as though nothing wrong had occurred. But it was far different with our hero, who passed a sleepless night of terror as to his probable fate on the morrow.

And when the morrow came, and he found himself in the dreaded presence of the constituted authority, armed with all the power of the law, he was so overcome, that he fell on his knees and made an abject spectacle of himself, imploring that he might not be expelled, and bring down his father's grey hairs in the usually quoted manner. To his immense relief, however, he was treated in a more lenient way; and as the term had nearly expired, his punishment could not be of long duration; and as for the impositions, why, as Mr. Bouncer said, 'Ain't there coves to *barber*ise 'em for you, Gig-lamps?'

Thus our freshman gained experience daily; so that by the end of the term, he found that short as the time had been, it had been long enough for him to learn what Oxford life was like, and that there was in it a great deal to be copied, as well as some things to be shunned. The freshness he had so freely shown on entering Oxford had gradually yielded as the term went on; and, when he had run halloing the Brazenface boat all the way up from Iffley, and had seen Mr. Blades realize his most sanguine dreams as to 'the head of the river;' and when, from the gallery of the theatre, he had taken part in the licensed saturnalia of the Commemoration, and had cheered for the ladies in pink and blue, and even given 'one more' for the very proctor who had so lately interfered with his liberties; and when he had gone to a farewell pass-party (which Charles Larkyns did *not* give), and had assisted in the other festivities that usually mark the end of the academical year, — Mr. Verdant Green found himself to be possessed of a considerable acquisition of knowledge of a most miscellaneous character; and on the authority, and in the figurative eastern language of Mr. Bouncer, 'he was sharpened up no end, by being well rubbed against university bricks. So, good-bye, old feller!' said the little gentleman, with a kind remembrance of imaginary individuals, 'and give my love to Sairey and the little uns.' And Mr. Bouncer 'went the complete unicorn,' for the last time in that term, by extemporising a farewell solo to Verdant, which was of such an agonizing character of execution, that Huz, and Buz his brother, lifted up their noses and howled.

'Which they're the very moral of Christyuns, sir!' observed Mrs. Tester, who was dabbing her curtseys in thankfulness for the large amount with which our hero had 'tipped' her. 'And has ears for moosic, sir. With grateful thanks to you, sir, for the same. And it's obleeged I feel in my art. Which it reelly were like what my own son would do, sir. As was found in drink for his rewing. And were took to the West Injies for a sojer. Which he were — ugh! oh, oh! Which you be'old me a hafflicted martyr to these spazzums, sir. And how I am to get through them doorin' the veecation. Without a havin' 'em eased by a-goin' to your cupboard, sir. For just three spots o' brandy on a lump o' sugar, sir. Is a summut as I'm afeered to think on. Oh! ugh!' Upon which Mrs. Tester's grief and spasms so completely overcame her, that our hero presented her with an extra half-sovereign, wherewith to purchase the medicine that was so peculiarly adapted to her complaint. Mr. Robert Filcher was also 'tipped' in the same liberal manner; and our hero completed his first term's residence in Brazenface by establishing himself as a decided favourite.

Among those who seemed disposed to join in this opinion was the Jehu of the Warwickshire coach, who expressed his conviction to our delighted hero, that 'he wos a young gent as had much himproved hisself since he tooled him up to the 'Varsity with his guvnor.' To fully deserve which high opinion, Mr. Verdant Green tipped for the box-seat, smoked more than was good for him, and besides finding the coachman in weeds, drank with him at every 'change' on the road.

The carriage met him at the appointed place, and his luggage (no longer encased in canvas, after the manner of females) was soon transferred to it; and away went our hero to the Manor Green, where he was received with the greatest demonstrations of delight. Restored to the bosom of his family, our hero was converted into a kind of domestic idol; while it was proposed by Miss Mary Green, seconded by Miss Fanny, and carried by unanimous acclamation, that Mr. Verdant Green's University career had greatly enhanced his attractions.

The opinion of the drawing-room was echoed from the servants'-hall, the ladies' maid in particular being heard freely to declare, that 'Oxford College had made quite a man of Master Verdant!'

As the little circumstance on which she probably grounded her encomium had fallen under the notice of Miss Virginia Verdant, it may have accounted for that most correct-minded lady being more reserved in expressing her opinion of her nephew's improvement than were the rest of the family; but she nevertheless thought a great deal on the subject.

'Well, Verdant!' said Mr. Green, after hearing divers anecdotes of his son's college-life, carefully prepared for home-consumption; 'now tell us what you've learnt in Oxford.'

'Why,' replied our hero, as he reflected on his freshman's career, 'I have learnt to think for myself, and not to believe every thing that I hear; and I think I could fight my way in the world; and I can chaff a cad — '

'Chaff a cad! oh!' groaned Miss Virginia to herself, thinking it was something extremely dreadful.

'And I have learnt to row — at least, not quite; but I can smoke a weed — a cigar, you know. I've learnt that.'

'Oh, Verdant, you naughty boy!' said Mrs. Green, with maternal fondness. 'I was sadly afraid that Charles Larkyns would teach you all his wicked school habits!'

'Why, mama,' said Mary, who was sitting on a footstool at her brother's knee, and spoke up in defence of his college friend; 'why, mama, all gentlemen smoke; and of course Mr. Charles Larkyns and Verdant must do as others do. But I dare say, Verdant, he taught you more useful things than that, did he not?'

'Oh, yes,' replied Verdant; 'he taught me to grill a devil.'

'Grill a devil!' groaned Miss Virginia.

185

'Infatuated young man!'

'And to make shandy-gaff and sherry-cobbler, and brew bishop and egg-flip: oh, it's capital! I'll teach you how to make it; and we'll have some to-night!'

And thus the young gentleman astonished his family with the extent of his learning, and proved how a youth of ordinary natural attainments may acquire other knowledge in his University career than what simply pertains to classical literature.

And so much experience had our hero gained during his freshman's term, that when the pleasures of the Long Vacation were at an end, and he had returned to Brazenface, with his firm and fast friend Charles Larkyns, he felt himself entitled to assume a patronizing air to the freshmen who then entered, and even sought to impose upon their credulity in ways which his own personal experience suggested.

It was clear that Mr. Verdant Green had made his farewell bow as an Oxford Freshman.

We do hope that you have enjoyed reading this large print book.

Did you know that all of our titles are available for purchase?

We publish a wide range of high quality large print books including:
Romances, Mysteries, Classics
General Fiction
Non Fiction and Westerns

Special interest titles available in large print are:
The Little Oxford Dictionary
Music Book
Song Book
Hymn Book
Service Book

Also available from us courtesy of Oxford University Press:
Young Readers' Dictionary
(large print edition)
Young Readers' Thesaurus
(large print edition)

For further information or a free brochure, please contact us at:
Ulverscroft Large Print Books Ltd.,
The Green, Bradgate Road, Anstey,
Leicester, LE7 7FU, England.
Tel: (00 44) 0116 236 4325
Fax: (00 44) 0116 234 0205

Other titles published by Ulverscroft:

GREY GRANITE

Lewis Grassic Gibbon

Widowed once again, Chris Colquohon has come to the industrial town of Duncairn, where life is as hard as the granite of the buildings all around her, and she must make her living as best she can by working in Ma Cleghorn's boarding house. Meanwhile, her son Ewan, forsaking his college career, finds employment at a steel manufacturer's, and determines to lead a peaceful strike against the manufacture of armaments. In the face of violence and police brutality, his socialist idealism is forged into something harder and fiercer as he readies himself to sacrifice all for the cause . . .

A TANGLED WEB

L. M. Montgomery

It all begins with Great Aunt Becky and her infamous prized possession: a legendary heirloom jug. After her death, everyone wants it. But the name of the new owner will not be revealed for one year ... Over the next twelve months, scandals, quarrels and love affairs abound within the Dark and Penhallow clans — with the jug at the centre of it all. Engagements are broken; lifelong mutual hatred blossoms into romance; lovers separated years ago are reunited. But then comes the night that the eccentric matriarch's wishes will be revealed - and both families are in for the biggest surprise of them all.

VICE VERSA

F. Anstey

Mr. Bultitude is unmoved by the pleading of his fourteen-year-old son Dick that he be spared from returning to Grimstone's tortuous boarding school. During his harangue on the free and easy life of youth, Mr. Bultitude unwisely expresses the wish that he himself might be a boy again — whilst clutching the magical Garudâ Stone, which is all too ready to oblige by transforming his outward appearance into that of his son's. To add insult to injury, Dick swiftly seizes the stone — and with it, the opportunity not only to assume his father's mature and portly form, but also gleefully pack Mr. Bultitude off to the hellish halls of Grimstone's . . .

THE AWAKENING

Kate Chopin

The Pontellier family are spending a hot, lazy holiday on the Gulf of Mexico. Nobody expects that Edna should be preoccupied with anything more than her husband Leonce and their small boys. But Edna, restive and achieving fulfilment only in her beloved sketching, finds her allocated bonds of motherhood and wifely duty to be stifling constraints. And when she teeters on the brink of an illicit summer romance with young clerk Robert Lebrun, new ideas and longings are awakened in her . . .

THE HAUNTED HOUSE

Charles Dickens & Hesba Stretton

In 1859, various literary luminaries — including Charles Dickens, Elizabeth Gaskell and Wilkie Collins — collaborated on a serialised work concerning events in a most peculiar house. This is their tale . . . When our narrator espies a deserted house from his railway carriage, he cannot resist the challenge of taking up residence in a place no one else will inhabit. Local legend has terrified the nearby villagers, who in turn convince his servants to abandon ship. Undaunted, he and his sister invite a group of friends to join them — each of whom is then commissioned to rout out the supernatural from their respective rooms. And come Twelfth Night, they will meet to recount their experiences . . .